Hunkered beside the freshly dug hole, Ethan stared up at me as I walked out. "Summer, you need to see this."

"What?"

"Uh." He ran a dirty hand through his curls. "I didn't kill your bush. Something clogged the drip line. The bush died of thirst. Take a look."

I peered into the dirt. The forgotten tumblers containing our drinks slipped from my hands. Sticky soda splattered my ankles.

About a foot down, a black velvet bag lay open. Dozens of diamonds sparkled, scattered among the deep brown dirt.

Don't miss out on a single one of our great mysteries. Contact us at the following address for information on our newest releases and club information:

Heartsong Presents—MYSTERIES! Readers' Service
PO Box 721
Uhrichsville, OH 44683
Web site: www.heartsongmysteries.com

Or for faster action, call 1-740-922-7280.

Fudge-Laced Felonies

A Summer Meadows Mystery

Cynthia Hickey

HEARTSONG
PRESENTS
MYSTERIES

First to God, who gives me a never-ending imagination and source of inspiration; my husband, Tom, my biggest fan and supporter; my agent, Kelly Mortimer, for believing in me; my editor, Susan Downs, for her encouragement; and my friend Dina McClain for pretty much daring me to write a first person cozy.

ISBN 978-1-60260-181-9

Cover Design: Kirk DouPonce, DogEared Design
Cover Illustration: Jody Williams

Our mission is to publish and distribute inspirational products offering exceptional value and biblical encouragement to the masses.

Printed in the U.S.A.

1

I marched into church on Sunday—not to search for God, but to find a killer.

My prey stood in the corner of the foyer, lurking in the shadows. With narrowed eyes, I intended to face him. Instead, the delicious aroma of coffee wafted in the air, beckoning me like a siren's song. I glared at the one I pursued long enough to let him know I meant business and switched my course across the tiled narthex of the large church to the fellowship wing. I needed caffeinated reinforcement before confronting the villain.

"Good morning, Summer." The barista, Susan, smiled and slid an ice-cold, mocha-flavored concoction into my waiting hands. "Thought you were going to pass us by."

"Not a chance." I nodded toward a man behind her. His back was turned, giving me a clear view of dark blue jeans beneath a navy apron. "Who's the new guy?"

Susan shrugged. "Nate something. I can't remember. He was here this morning when I got in. Seems like a nice enough kind of guy. Quiet." She winked. "Very handsome."

"Not interested." Pursing my lips around the straw, I closed my eyes, giving in to the sheer bliss of the drink. Immediately, the coffee seized my brain in a painful grip of ice. My eyes shot open.

Susan smiled. "I've told you a thousand times not to gulp it."

I pinched the bridge of my nose between my thumb

and forefinger. Pressure released, I turned, focusing again on the man I'd come to confront.

"Leave him alone, Summer." Susan handed me a napkin.

What? Did everyone know what he'd done?

"You're glaring at Ethan like you want to put a hole through him."

"He's a murderer, and I intend to see justice served." Righteous indignation rose in my chest, and my face grew warm. My fair skin probably burned as scarlet as a summer sunset. I ducked my head and took another long suck on the straw, drawing strength from the frozen coffee.

Ethan Banning, murderer extraordinaire—looking as fine as Adonis in khaki pants and a baby blue polo shirt—emerged from his routine of greeting the arriving parishioners. A wide, white smile and dimples you could drown in had probably sent many a woman's heart into palpitations. I steeled myself to resist his charms as I approached him.

"Good morning, Summer." His deep voice rolled over me like faraway thunder on a spring day.

With tremendous willpower, I forced myself not to fall into his deep blue eyes and instead focused on a spot over his shoulder. Big mistake. He stepped closer, and I caught a whiff of some heavenly men's cologne.

"It's not a good morning, Ethan." I stepped back. "You're a murderer." I lowered my voice to a whisper. "I can't believe the people of this church trust their youth to you. I'll never allow you to care for any of my children."

"Got your Irish dander up again, don't you?" Ethan laughed. "You don't have any children."

I met his gaze. The drink in my hand sweated, the

condensation running down my arm. "Well, if I did, I—"

Taking hold of my arm, Ethan pulled me away from the throng of people. "I'm sorry I killed your rosebush, Summer, but I did warn you I don't have a green thumb."

"But you're a teacher, Ethan. I trusted you."

"I'm not a gardener." He dropped his hand. "Why aren't you at the child check booth?"

"It's my month off." I felt a stab of pity at the frustrated look on his face.

"Look. We'll go by the nursery after church and I'll buy you another rosebush. Meet me out front."

"The Midnight Blue? They're hard to find. And expensive."

"Yes. Whatever you want." He turned to smile at a middle-aged woman. "Good morning, Mrs. Parker. How are you this beautiful, sunny day?"

"Oh, I'm fine, Ethan. Now that my son has come home."

They released Duane from prison? I racked my brain trying to remember the boy I'd gone to school with. The boy I'd rejected as a prom date. Then he'd been sent to prison for assault, and I'd counted my blessings for not getting hooked up with him. Ethan took the woman's arm, said something soft, and stepped away. The sun, once streaming through the large front windows, hid behind a cloud, casting me in shadow.

With a sigh, I flounced past Ethan to attend the second morning service, faltering as he called to me. "Pay close attention to this morning's sermon, Summer. It's on forgiveness." At the sound of Ethan's laughter rumbling across the foyer, my spine stiffened.

Sitting in the pew, I tried to focus on the pastor's words, but images of my shriveled rosebush wouldn't go away. I'd only been gone for three days! How could anyone kill a thriving plant in three days?

I gazed at the stained-glass windows. One in particular grabbed my attention. The rose of Sharon. I closed my eyes in mental anguish, letting my head fall back against the pew. I took the hard *thunk* of skull meeting wood as a sign of God telling me to pay attention. Straightening, I refocused my thoughts on the pastor's words.

"'And when you stand praying, if you hold anything against anyone, forgive him, so that your Father in heaven may forgive you your sins.'"

Flipping in my Bible to Mark 11:25, I reread the words and groaned inwardly. I wasn't ready to forgive Ethan. I'd loved that rosebush. Well, I loved it as much as anyone can love a nonhuman object, and I'd had high hopes.

Once I'd decided to grow flowers for the town's annual rose festival, I'd searched for the perfect one. I'd special ordered the Midnight Blue and waited weeks for it to arrive. I hoped Uncle Roy's nursery had ordered more than one. The exhibit loomed, now only months away.

I'm sorry, Lord. Thank You for Your words. I'll do better. I will. I forgive Ethan—but he'd better buy me another rosebush.

True to his word, Ethan waited in front of the church, truck door held gallantly open. "We'll pick your car up later."

"Why can't we take it now?" The wind blew beneath the flirty skirt I wore, causing me to yelp. I struggled to hold the garment in place and not expose my assets to the man I least desired to embarrass myself in front of. Being the gentleman he is, Ethan turned his head, but not before he smirked.

"It'll be easier if we take my truck. We'll have somewhere to put the bush." He closed the door and loped to the driver's side. "How's the business going? Ready to open?"

"Fine." I smoothed the skirt into place over my bird legs. At least they weren't fat, as my aunt always told me. "Aunt Eunice and I are doing a good job of marketing. I expect a prosperous opening day."

"Really? That's great!" He drove around the parking lot, too slow for my taste, stopping to greet and wish a good day to everyone we passed. "Is there much money in chocolate?"

"Not just chocolate, Ethan." How could someone so handsome be so dense? "Hand-dipped candies made with the finest ingredients."

"Don't get testy." He steered onto the street. "I'm just making conversation."

"I think you deliberately antagonize me. You've done it since we were in grade school."

The corner of his mouth twitched. "But it's so much fun. Why do you try to disguise your red hair? 'Cause with that temper of yours—"

I pulled my hair over my shoulder, admiring the rich auburn color that came only from a bottle. "Don't tease me about my orange hair."

"Your hair isn't orange. A beautiful red laced with gold. Like molten lava."

"Oh, and now you're a poet?" I smirked, tossing my

hair over my shoulder.

"Aspiring poet."

It didn't take long to drive across Mountain Shadows, Arkansas. Population: 27,000. Fifteen minutes after leaving church, Ethan pulled into the parking lot of the only garden nursery in the city.

I sat with my back ramrod straight and waited for Ethan to open my door. I expected him to treat me like the lady I knew myself to be. I smoothed the crisp cotton of the white skirt over my thighs.

"My lady." Ethan flung the door open and bowed.

How does he do that? The man always seems to know what I'm thinking. "Thank you." I stepped primly from the truck, nose in the air. My foot sank into a hole. I cried out as I toppled off my high heel and clutched at Ethan.

He grabbed my arm. "You okay? You should really watch where you're going, Summer. That pothole was clearly visible."

"I'm fine." Yanking my arm free, I limped past him with a throbbing ankle and preceded him through the wrought iron gates of the nursery. His laughter didn't improve my mood.

"Buying another rosebush already, Summer?" Roy Meadows, my uncle and owner of the nursery, wiped his hands on the thighs of his coveralls.

"I have to. Ethan killed the poor thing. While you, me, and Aunt Eunice were in Branson. Didn't you see it this morning when you left the house? Please tell me you have another Midnight Blue."

"As a matter of fact, I do." He held a soil-encrusted hand out to Ethan. "Sounds like you're in hot water, mister."

Ethan didn't seem to notice the dirt beneath my uncle's fingernails. He returned the hearty handshake. "I sure am. I'll be paying for the new bush for a long time to come. And I'm not talking about money."

Roy laughed. "Yep. That's my Summer. She may be beautiful, but her tongue is as sharp as a brand-new garden hoe. She might just be the sassiest girl in these Ozark foothills."

"If y'all are finished ridiculing me, we really need to get this rosebush planted sometime today." I did enjoy a moment of pleasure when he called me beautiful, and I glanced at Ethan to see whether he'd noticed my uncle's flattery for his only niece. Apparently he didn't. The two men set off without me.

Regretting my choice of footwear for the second time that day, I limped after them, stepping over stretched hoses and hobbling around garden tools. My uncle wasn't organized.

A man stepped from behind a toolshed and wiped his hands on the front of his navy coveralls. I recognized the bully from high school. He couldn't hide behind a bushy dark beard.

"Duane!" My uncle waved him over. "You remember my niece, Summer, don't you?"

Duane nodded without smiling.

Uncle Roy turned back to Ethan and me. "Duane's working for me now. Good worker. Doesn't talk much, keeps to himself. . . Lives in the trailer park down by the railroad tracks. You know the one. Not too far from our place. You've probably heard him whistling as he takes his nightly walks." Sometimes Uncle Roy started talking and rambled on and on. Why couldn't he just get to the

Midnight Blue? "Ah, here she is." He pointed to a five-gallon bucket of lush emerald leaves.

"Yay!" I clapped my hands together. "Let's get her loaded in Ethan's truck."

The men looked at me as if I'd turned green.

"Let's? You plan on helping, sweetie?" My uncle turned to me, his brow furrowed. " 'Cause it'll be the first time. Or I could send Duane over?"

"I planted the last bush, Uncle Roy." My cheeks burned with such intensity that they hurt. Along with my bruised feelings. "I've planted all my rosebushes myself. I'm not afraid of getting my hands dirty."

Uncle Roy winked at Ethan. "She wears a pair of pink gardening gloves, and she has these flowered overalls." He shook his head. "I haven't the faintest idea where she gets that stuff. But she makes a purty picture."

I rolled my eyes and folded my arms across my chest. From now on, moving out of Uncle Roy's place and getting my own home was going to be a priority.

"Okay, Summer, we'll get going." Ethan's arms bulged beneath his polo shirt as he hefted the bucket onto a nearby dolly. "I'd like to enjoy some of my Sunday."

"I do appreciate this," I told him. "I can plant the bush myself if you have other things to do." *Please say you'll plant it. Don't leave so soon.*

"I'll plant it. After all, I was responsible for its predecessor's death." My heart leaped with the abandon of a young colt.

Two minutes later, Ethan pulled into the driveway, crunching gravel. I swung open the truck door and slid from the seat. "I'll pour us some cold drinks."

As I limped up the porch steps and unlocked the door,

I glanced back. Ethan was dragging the rosebush from the truck bed. The sun shone on his head, highlighting his blond curls with a halo. I sighed from the sheer beauty of the picture he made then opened the door.

The scraping of the shovel along with gentle thuds of dirt hitting the ground floated through the open kitchen window. I peeked out and caught a glance at the back of Ethan's head as he stretched, his hands braced against his lower back.

"I'll be right out!" I poured soda into a plastic tumbler. Pushing open the screen door, I stepped into the afternoon sun. My cairn terrier, Truly Scrumptious, squeezed past my legs and shot into the yard.

Hunkered beside the freshly dug hole, Ethan stared up at me as I walked out. "Summer, you need to see this."

"What?"

"Uh." He ran a dirty hand through his curls. "I didn't kill your bush. Something clogged the drip line. The bush died of thirst. Take a look."

I peered into the dirt. The forgotten tumblers containing our drinks slipped from my hands. Sticky soda splattered my ankles. About a foot down, a black velvet bag lay open.

Dozens of diamonds sparkled, scattered among the deep brown dirt.

My breath caught, and I put my hand to my throat. My heart raced.

"I'm rich."

I thought I'd mouthed the words silently, but apparently not, because Ethan glared at me.

"You can't keep them." He stood, wiping his hands on the seat of his pants. "Any idea how they got here?"

"Well, I don't think they're Uncle Roy's." I squatted and ran my fingers through the precious stones, reveling in the cool feel of wealth. "Why would someone bury diamonds beneath my Midnight Blue?" I lifted the drip line and scooped out a stone with the nail of my pinky. The sun shot glimmers of color through the diamond's facets. Sighing, I let the jewel fall back with the others.

Ethan shrugged and held out a hand to help me to my feet. "The ground was already soft. If someone was in a hurry and spotted your freshly planted rosebush, then—"

I accepted his offered hand, glorying in the feel of its roughness covering my own. "Are you sure I can't keep them? Finders keepers and all that?"

"Positive, Summer."

Behind us, a vehicle roared into the drive. My plump, white-haired aunt opened the door to the 1965 Chevy pickup and bounded out. Aunt Eunice did everything fast. My uncle called her the White Tornado. She might be short and round, but she had the energy of a skinny woman. "What y'all looking at?"

"Come see." I beckoned her, smiling at the way Aunt Eunice's cheeks jiggled when she walked.

She shoved her glasses farther up on her nose and planted chubby fists on even chubbier hips. "Whooee! You two fertilizing with diamonds now?"

"Don't be silly." I bumped her with a hip. "We didn't put them there."

"Then who did?" She squinted up at Ethan. "You call the po-lice yet?"

"We just found them. I was about to plant Summer's new rosebush." He used his forearm to wipe the perspiration from his brow.

"Won't be no planting it now." Aunt Eunice turned to me. "Better find another place for your rosebush, Summer. I don't think Roy will place another 'emergency' order for you if you don't get that one into the ground."

Truly nosed around the other bushes. She made snuffling noises as she traveled with her muzzle to the ground. She let out a bark and started digging beneath my recently planted coral heirloom roses. Were none of my bushes sacred?

"Truly, stop that!" I took a small step away from the fresh hole, hesitant to venture farther than a couple of feet, the glittering diamonds entrancing me with shimmering rainbows of light. "You're ruining my heirlooms!"

The feisty little terrier snarled as her front paws hurled dirt and mulch from beneath her body. Within seconds, she shook a dirty piece of cloth in her mouth. I pounced, released from the trance of the sparkling jewels, and grabbed the material from the dog's mouth.

"Ugh!" I let the garden glove fall to the ground. Russet brown covered the palm. "Is that blood?"

"Don't touch anything." Ethan appeared, his bottom lip between his teeth as he bent over the offending object. "Do you think it could be?"

"That's not one of my gloves." Planting my hands on my hips, I made a slow turn, my eyes searching the trees around my aunt and uncle's property. But why would someone bury a bloody glove in one hole and diamonds in another? And why beneath my rosebushes? I spotted a shovel tossed to the side. "And why is Uncle Roy's shovel out of the shed? He'd never do that."

"There's more." While I'd searched the bushes, Ethan poked his foot at something beneath the bush where we'd discovered the glove. A rusty coffee can lay half buried in the dirt. "Look."

"*That's* where he stashed it." Eunice snatched the can from the hole and pulled off the plastic lid. Inside lay a tightly bound roll of cash.

"Who's 'he'?" My eyes widened at the bundle of bills.

"Your uncle. This here can holds our cruise money. You know how much I've always wanted to take a cruise." A smug smile spread across my aunt's face. "Roy thought he was being so clever."

"Uncle Roy hid your cruise money with a glove?" I couldn't believe it. I knew my aunt and uncle were a unique pair, but this was beyond even them.

"You'll have to ask your uncle about that." Eunice hugged the can to her chest. "Now, where can I hide it?"

Ethan stared from me to my aunt, his mouth hanging

open. He clamped it closed then opened it again to speak. "You shouldn't have picked up the can. I'm going in to call Joe. You two do whatever it is you two do."

"Ask him to stay for supper," Aunt Eunice blurted once Ethan disappeared into the house.

"What?"

"Ask him to stay for supper," Eunice repeated. "The boy's been working hard all day." She turned and nosed around the yard, peering beneath trees and bushes, apparently searching for the perfect hiding place.

Wanting to be wherever Ethan was, I called for the dog to follow and traced Ethan's steps into the house. I glanced out the window as my uncle rumbled up the drive in his truck, which matched Aunt Eunice's. My aunt shrieked.

She danced around, holding the can above her head. She reminded me of an ancient warrior princess in some weird ritual. I giggled. Ethan shook his head and lifted the phone receiver.

The afternoon sun came through the kitchen window, highlighting the light stubble on his chin. My gaze roamed to his mouth. I jerked away. What if he caught me staring at his lips? I'd be mortified. No matter that he looked thoroughly kissable. Even with streaks of dirt on his face. And no matter that ever since junior high, I've wondered what it would feel like to have Ethan Banning kiss me.

"What? Do I have dirt on my face?"

"Huh?" My cheeks heated.

"Dirt. On my face. You're staring." He narrowed his eyes. "Did you get sunburned today?"

Horror. "Yes. No. Dirt. Right there." I pointed to a spot above his nose. I opened my mouth to say something witty to save myself from further embarrassment, but someone apparently picked up the phone on the other end, because Ethan started speaking.

"Hello. This is Ethan Banning. May I speak with Officer Parson, please? Yeah. Joe, there's a problem at the Meadowses' place. We've found a couple of things you should take a look at. . . . No, I think you should come over. Looks to be a bloody glove and a whole lot of diamonds. Okay." Ethan hung up then glanced at his watch. "He'll be here in about fifteen minutes."

He lifted those gorgeous cobalt blue eyes of his to look at me, and I almost forgot what Aunt Eunice wanted me to ask him. "Uh. My aunt told me to invite you to an early dinner."

"She did, huh?" A dimple appeared in Ethan's right cheek. "Is that why you've been staring at me?"

"Of course." I swallowed hard. No way could I let him know how I felt about him. My friend April, Ethan's sister, knew; she thought it stupid of me not to say anything, but Ethan always treated me like a younger sister.

Since I'd first laid eyes on him the summer I turned ten and Ethan fifteen, I've been stark raving mad about him. Then he went away to college and returned a couple of years ago. I've never found the right time to open my mouth and spill out my feelings.

"I'd love to. Do you think Eunice would mind if April came? Since our parents went to heaven, we usually spend Sunday together."

"I'm sure she wouldn't." Great. Ethan had never stayed for dinner before, and now April would be all eyes on the two of us. A smug grin on her pretty round face.

The screen door banged against the wall with a loud crack as Aunt Eunice and Uncle Roy stormed inside. Uncle Roy stepped back as Aunt Eunice shoved past him, the coffee can still clutched in her hands. She slammed the can on the Formica-topped kitchen table.

"This isn't our can." She folded her arms across her ample bosom, her face creased. "Roy said he hasn't seen it before. And he won't tell me where he hid our cruise money. Did you call the po-lice yet?"

"I did. Joe will be here soon." Ethan took a step away, his gaze glued to the rusty coffee can. "So, someone buried diamonds beneath one rosebush. Money and a glove beneath another. The question is, why here?"

"Don't forget this someone killed Summer's rose-bush." Aunt Eunice nodded, her lips set in a straight line.

I stared at my aunt as if she'd sprouted antennae. I'd always thought of myself as an amateur sleuth, having grown up reading Agatha Christie and Nancy Drew. The thought of a mystery of this magnitude raised goose bumps on my arms. Killed my rosebush? Amazingly, I no longer cared about the bush.

"Uh-oh." Ethan shook his head. "I recognize the gleam in Summer's eyes. She can't wait to sink her teeth into this."

"I just want to find out why someone chose our yard to bury the diamonds and cash in. What if someone is trying to frame us somehow? You can help me, Ethan. It'll be like old times." *Before you went away to college. And, maybe, if I solve this case, you'll see me as something other than the empty-headed little girl who used to follow you around.*

I leaned against the counter. Excitement bubbled

inside me like sparkling cider. "Remember when someone stole my bike? I investigated and found out a mean kid down the block took it, and then you went and got the bike back."

"This isn't the same thing." Ethan pulled a wooden chair away from the table, and its legs shrieked against the linoleum floor. "We have something more valuable than a banana seat bike. We have diamonds, money, and possibly a bloody glove."

Uh-oh. I recognized the tone in his voice. Ethan would try to stop me.

"I agree, Summer." Uncle Roy pulled out another chair and squeezed his bulk onto it, the wood protesting beneath him. "This isn't a game. Could be dangerous."

"I'm perfectly capable of"—a car pulled into the driveway, and I glanced out the window—"solving such a simple mystery. You know how small towns are. People will think I stole the—" A handsome man in a tan officer's uniform sat behind the wheel of a squad car.

Matchmaking reared its lovely head. Maybe I could get my cousin, Joe, to stay for dinner, too. He and April could get better acquainted. Why should I be the only one mooning over a guy?

The officer's shoulders slumped as he made his way to the porch. Aunt Eunice bustled toward the door and flung it open, her cheeks rosy from the day's events. "Good afternoon, Joe. How's your Sunday?"

Joe removed his hat and stepped inside. "Wish I could say things were better. Y'all found a glove and diamonds?"

"Yes." Aunt Eunice pointed to the table. "And a can full of money."

Joe frowned as his gaze flicked to the can. "You touched it?"

"I thought it might be the money Roy's been hiding for our cruise. The old coot doesn't want me to spend it." Aunt Eunice tossed her husband a frustrated look.

"Where are the diamonds?" Joe ran a hand through his hair.

"Out here." Ethan rose, shook Joe's hand, and then led the group back into the yard. Despite myself, I couldn't help but compare the two men.

Ethan stood tall, slender, and muscled, like a jungle cat, whereas Joe stood shorter than Ethan's six feet four by several inches. Stocky, built more like a bear. I recalled how Ethan towered over me during my high school years, teasing me because of my five-foot-two-inch frame. He called me Tinkerbell. I'd hated it, even as I longed for him.

3

The two men stared into the freshly dug hole, looking like a pair of mismatched bookends. Both placed their hands on their hips. Then Joe changed the picture by squatting and lifting a sparkling diamond from the dirt.

"Well, look at that." He held the stone high. The sun's rays cast bolts of light through the stone, and my materialistic heart leaped. "Ain't that a pretty sight." He dropped the diamond and straightened, brushing the dirt from his hands by rubbing them together. "Summer, when's the grand opening?"

"Tomorrow." Summer Confections opened in the morning, and my excitement knew no bounds. I'd wanted to open my own candy store for years. Now my dream would become a reality.

"I'll be there." Joe elbowed Ethan. "Summer can stand a little sweetening now, can't she?"

"More than a little," Ethan replied then laughed, sounding more like a great baboon with each chuckle.

My euphoria diminished with the speed of a bullet. With what I hoped was a classy tilt of my chin, I turned. "Very funny." And with those cutting words, I marched back into the house.

I parted the white, lacy café-style curtains and glared out the window at the two men. Their faded murmurs reached my ears through the glass. Ethan caught me watching and winked. I clamped my lips together and dropped the curtains back into place.

"Don't let it bother you, honey." Aunt Eunice joined me in the kitchen and pulled open the refrigerator door. She removed a glass pitcher of what I knew would be the sweetest tea in the South. "This will sweeten you up." She giggled, clearly proud of herself. "Sorry, Summer. I couldn't resist. Ethan don't mean nothing by it."

I accepted the glass of tea. "Can I ask you something, Aunt Eunice?"

The older woman plopped with a sigh into the nearest kitchen chair. "You sure can."

"What's wrong with me?"

"Wrong?" My aunt lifted her glass to her lips.

"Why can't I get a man to settle into a relationship with me?" I sighed, feeling as if a great burden rested on my shoulders.

"You scare them. Men, I mean." With precision, Aunt Eunice set her glass on the tabletop. "You're beautiful, you're smart, and, forgive me for saying so, you're rather spoiled." She exhaled and relaxed. "There. I've finally said it."

"Spoiled?" *Finally said it? What? She's been bottling that thought inside?* I scratched my head, seriously unsure of how to respond. I'd held down jobs of different sorts since the age of sixteen, and tomorrow I'd unlock the door to my own candy store. I couldn't be spoiled.

Aunt Eunice held up a hand. "Don't take this wrong, Summer, but your Uncle Roy and I haven't used the word *no* much in the years we've raised you. That silly old man out there always would give you anything you wanted if it was within his power to do so. That left you a little spoiled. Your expectations are set too high. That scares off most men."

She turned toward the window. The men's silhouettes danced on the opposite side of the pane. "And if you don't get those stars out of your eyes every time you look at Ethan, he's going to figure out your true feelings."

"It's that noticeable?" My hand flew to cover my heart. "I've been so careful to hide how I feel."

"Not careful enough, Summer." The screen door squeaked as April waltzed inside and planted a kiss on my aunt's cheek. "I hope y'all don't mind that I barged on in. The door was open."

Aunt Eunice's chair screeched as she pushed it back. "Not at all, sweetie. Our door is always open to you and your brother. He's outside with Joe right now, playing with diamonds."

April's eyes, so like her brother's, gleamed. "Diamonds?"

"Somebody dumped a bunch of diamonds beneath my Midnight Blue. Oh, and some cash and a bloody glove, too." I waved a hand, trying to make light of April's question about the diamonds.

Not careful? Could it be that obvious? The dreaded heat of embarrassment crept up my neck. *How would I ever face him again?* Quick. Something to take my mind off things. I scanned the kitchen, and because I possessed the type of luck that gave me the exact opposite of what I hoped for, Ethan and Joe pushed through the door.

"Ethan Banning!" April put her hands on her straight hips. "You didn't tell me anything about diamonds." She turned a thousand-watt smile in Joe's direction. "Joe?"

The big man turned several shades of red. "Uh. Hi, April." He scratched his head and sent a pleading look toward Ethan. And him, a police officer—thrown speechless at a pretty girl's question.

I decided to help my aunt serve dinner as April scolded the men about keeping secrets from her. With much protesting, they situated themselves around the table. Once everyone was seated, I jumped to my feet to grab the pan of corn bread. My sandal caught on the chair rung, and I fell into Ethan.

His big hands encircled my waist. Positive I'd now break out in hives, I froze. "Summer? You okay?"

Just fine. My heart beat so fast my chest hurt, and I couldn't breathe from the humiliation. But other than that, things were just peachy. "I'm fine. Sorry."

April snorted behind her hand, and I shot her the frostiest look I could muster. Ethan glanced between the two of us. I held my breath, fearful of April spilling my secret.

Joe rose from his chair. "Can't stay for more than a drink of your fine tea, Eunice." He lifted a glass to her. "I need to get this evidence back to the office."

"Even policemen have to eat, Joe."

He shook his head and slapped his hat on his head. "The scene's been contaminated enough already. Best I get people working on where these diamonds came from."

"Don't forget the bloody glove." Aunt Eunice placed a bowl of spaghetti on the table.

I stared at the red sauce poured over noodles. My stomach churned, and my breathing resembled that of a woman in Lamaze class. If I were going to solve this case, I'd need to be made of stronger stuff. I doubted Miss Marple got queasy at the thought of blood.

I placed a bowl of warm bread on the table, spreading a tantalizing aroma through the kitchen. I counted off what I knew about the crime, which wasn't much.

One, there are diamonds. Lots of the little beauties. Two, cash. I didn't know how much because I hadn't counted it, but I planned on finding out. Third, the bloody glove. Saturated glove, really. Way too much for a simple gardening injury. My traitorous stomach soured. Did someone lie dead, brutally murdered, waiting to be discovered? The thought made my skin crawl.

I left the dining area and followed Joe out the front door, skipping to keep up with his long stride. "Joe. How much cash was in the can?"

He stopped, turned, and studied me with his brown eyes. "Why do you want to know, Summer?"

"Just curious." I flashed him what I hoped was a beguiling dimple. "I could ask my uncle. I know he counted, but he tends to exaggerate."

"Around one thousand dollars, according to Roy." He spun on his heel and marched toward his squad car. "Save the coyness for Ethan. And don't get in my way."

One thousand dollars! Plus the diamonds. As best I could figure at this point, someone wore the gardening gloves while they fought over the diamonds and money. And, very possibly, someone had died. Goose bumps rose on my arms.

My gaze fell on the Sunday morning newspaper still lying in the driveway. Having missed the gift of patience, I needed to start somewhere. If there wasn't a story on the front page about a murder, reading the obituaries seemed a logical choice. There was bound to be somebody listed who'd died of unnatural causes. Maybe even on the front page!

By the time I reentered the room, Uncle Roy had

joined the group. The talking and laughter grew loud. I paused in the doorway, soaking in the scene. Gathered around the table, enjoying each other's company, sat the people I loved most in the world. The verse in the Bible about breaking bread and sharing fellowship took on a whole new meaning for me. A lump rose in my throat, and I blinked away tears.

"Ain't ya going to eat, Summer?" Aunt Eunice asked, her fork suspended halfway between her mouth and the plate. "Is something ailing you?"

"I brought in the paper." I tossed it on the counter and sat down. April raised her eyebrows and shoveled a forkful of spaghetti into her mouth. Fine. I usually didn't bring in the paper, and I never read it, but there's always a first time. I shrugged at my friend.

"Aunt Eunice, I was thinking about that gardening glove."

"Uh-oh, here we go." Ethan's fork clattered against his plate.

I glared at him before continuing. "I'm going to check the obituaries after lunch and follow up on any non-natural deaths."

"Non-natural?"

"Yeah. You know, like unnatural causes. Could be one of those people is our victim."

"I think you need to stay out of it. There may not even be a victim." Ethan leaned back in his chair. "This is Joe's business. His line of work. He'll know if something shady is going on. You should stick to making candy."

My eyes narrowed. Stick to making candy, indeed! I'd solve this case just to prove something to Mr. Banning, and I'd have Aunt Eunice help me. April, too. I'd show him what a few women could do.

"Now, don't go getting your dander up." Uncle Roy wiped his mouth on the napkin he'd tucked into the neckline of his overalls and tossed the wadded paper onto his empty plate. "I agree with Ethan. This might be dangerous. Besides, if you're running around the county investigating dead people, you won't be able to make money at the candy store."

"And," Aunt Eunice added. "If we don't make money at the store, I'll have to go back to breeding Chihuahuas or something."

"I thought you were on my side, Aunt Eunice."

"It ain't about taking sides, sweetie."

"Fine." I scooted my chair back and stood. "I'll do it myself." Snatching the newspaper from the counter, I stalked out the kitchen door, letting it slam behind me.

Skimming the obituaries turned out to be a rather grisly way to spend a few minutes on a Sunday, and I didn't find a single person who'd died a violent death. I let the paper fall to the wood floor of the porch and lazily swung my foot, sending the swing into a restful back-and-forth motion.

Laughter floated on the breeze, coming through the screen. The warm spring sun caressed the bare skin of my legs. My eyelids grew heavy. Grabbing an old pillow, I slid sideways and cradled my head.

The rustle of the newspaper woke me. I opened my eyes and lifted a hand to shade them. Ethan shook the paper, his eyes reading over the page I'd left out.

"Obituaries, Summer? I thought you were kidding." Blue eyes bored into mine.

I sat up, shrugged, then set the swing back into

motion. "It's a good place to start."

"Why are you set on solving this? Isn't the candy store going to give you enough to do?" Ethan stopped the swing long enough to join me.

"Why did someone choose my rosebush? Whoever did got me involved."

Ethan laid his arm across the back of the swing. My breath hitched at his closeness. "This isn't the same as trying to locate a missing bike." He shifted to stare at me. "A bloody gardening glove isn't child's play. Let Joe handle it."

"Worried about me?"

He ruffled my hair, and I scowled. "Of course. Wouldn't want anything to happen to my Tinkerbell." He rose and handed me the paper. "Good luck on your opening tomorrow."

"Thanks." He left, and the day grew suddenly cooler without his presence. I shivered.

I woke suddenly. My eyes snapped open, my heart in my throat, as I peered through the darkness of my room. What had I heard? A board creaking? The house shifting? Truly growled from the foot of my bed. I grasped the sheet in both hands and yanked it to my chin.

There! A scrape on the stairs. I rose to a sitting position. My brave canine launched herself at me, still barking, and scurried to hide behind me.

"Shh." I held my breath and laid a hand on the dog's neck. "Stay." I slid my legs over the side of the bed then stood, trembling, ears strained.

With slow, cautious steps, I made my way to the door and peered around the corner. The empty hallway stretched before me. The oak wood floor, darkened by the shadows, looked a country mile long and as sinister as an inner-city block.

I craned my neck until I could spot the closed door of my aunt and uncle's room. Another groan from a loose board, and I whipped around.

A silhouette stretched across the wall, moving down the corridor. Truly's barking grew into a frenzy as a dark-clothed figure stepped into my line of sight. The figure spun, bolting in the opposite direction.

"Hey! Stop!"

Heart pounding, I grabbed a wooden baseball bat that leaned against the wall and the cell phone from its charger on my nightstand. I punched in 911 and took off after the prowler. My bare feet slapped against the floor. I held my nightgown wadded in one hand to prevent it tangling around my knees as I raced down the stairs.

"Uncle Roy! Intruder!"

Truly shot between my legs, causing me to trip as she launched her little body toward the fleeing suspect. My knees hit with a bone-jarring *thud*. I braced myself with my hands and raised my head.

My growling canine slid into a corner after receiving a well-aimed kick from the fleeing figure. I pushed to my feet and scooped Truly into my arms.

Within moments, the dark figure disappeared. Standing in the empty living room, holding a shuddering dog, I stared into the night. My hand rubbed Truly's coarse fur. The action served to calm me, slowing my racing heart.

"What is it?" Uncle Roy lurched into the room, a shotgun held in front of him.

"There was someone here. Upstairs." I stepped over to the door and studied it.

My stomach quivered as I ran my fingers over the splintered wood around the ancient lock. "Probably should've changed these locks last month when I suggested it, Uncle Roy."

He squinted, his face turned toward the yard. "I said I'd get to it one of these days. I guess tomorrow's that day."

Keeping his gun ready, he stepped forward. "Did you call 911? Who was it? How many were there?" He turned to glare at me with narrowed eyes. "What are you doing chasing an intruder anyway? That's a man's work. You should've waited for me." Uncle Roy made a motion with his gun.

I looked at the phone in my hand. In my haste, I hadn't turned it on. "I didn't call yet, and I didn't see a weapon." When did he think I would've had the time? "I don't know, and I saw one person. It isn't like I left the house after them." I stepped off the porch, joining him. The cool blades of grass tickled my feet. "The person dressed in bulky clothes. It could have been a woman. Maybe even a man."

"A woman?" Uncle Roy transferred his attention back to me. "Whatever for?"

"The diamonds?" I bent and released the dog. Truly scampered away with her nose to the ground. "The person wasn't very big. If I hadn't tripped over the dog, I'd have caught him or her."

"And then what? We sent the diamonds and the cash

with Joe." Uncle Roy lowered his rifle. "Don't make no sense, Summer. Anybody with any brains would know we didn't keep the stuff."

I shrugged. "They were looking for something else, then." A shudder ran down my spine. "Maybe there's more somewhere."

"More what?"

Lowering my voice to a whisper, I said, "More diamonds. Or money." I again hitched up my nightgown and bolted around the corner of the house. "Beneath one of the other rosebushes, maybe."

Uncle Roy followed. "You're not digging up the rosebushes at"—he glanced at his watch—"two thirty in the morning. It's too dangerous, and you have a big day ahead of you. A day you've waited for a long time."

"But—"

"I'll phone Joe, since you haven't. Let him know somebody broke into our house. You get ready for your grand opening."

The moon lit up the backyard like a magical fairyland, and I made my way to where my dying Midnight Blue bush stood with wilting branches. Its new twin stood proudly a couple of feet away. In the moistened dirt beneath the rosebushes were clear footprints.

I placed my foot next to the print. "Look, Uncle Roy. Whoever's been here has much bigger feet than me."

"The kid down the street has bigger feet than you, honey. Look at this mark. Someone knelt down right here. I'll go call Joe. This time I mean it." He turned and went into the house.

As I backed up, it occurred to me the prowler might be watching from the oak trees bordering the property, and I was vulnerable. With a sudden revelation of my stupidity, I turned and ran to the safety of the kitchen.

———

After the police finished casing the scene, I dragged my tired body up the stairs.

Sleep eluded me the rest of the early morning hours. I lay in bed, staring through the morning darkness toward the ceiling overhead. Soft murmurs drifted through the wall from where Uncle Roy obviously translated the morning's happenings to Aunt Eunice.

I flopped from my back to my side. I really needed rest. My eyes were gritty. The alarm clock numbers shone red. Four thirty. I groaned.

The previous day's events clicked through my mind like a slide show, beginning with my first sighting of Ethan at church and ending with the last hour. Dismay washed over me. I always wanted quick results, yet I hadn't been able to garner a single clue. Miss Marple I wasn't.

Would the thief be at the store's opening? Could it be a resident of Mountain Shadows, or someone new? Was the night prowler the thief returning for the diamonds or something more sinister? Had I offended anyone? Ethan had been with me when we discovered the jewels. Did that mean anything? Moaning, I pounded the pillow.

"You all right, Summer?" Aunt Eunice called from the other side of the thin wall.

"I'm fine. Sorry." I clenched my fists to prevent myself from whacking the pillow again and remembered what the pastor said once when he'd had trouble sleeping.

He prayed for others. Mentally, I ran down the list of family and friends, praying for whoever came to mind. But images of blood-spattered diamonds and menacing figures in black kept interrupting me, rolling across the front of my brain. What had I gotten myself into?

4

"Good morning!" Aunt Eunice sang as she tossed aside the window curtains. "We had a bit of excitement last night, didn't we?"

Pulling the sheet over my face, I groaned. "Why are you so chipper?"

"We're alive, the sun is shining, and God is in heaven. Plus, despite being woken at an ungodly hour by an intruder, we're safe. No one was harmed. Why shouldn't I be happy? Besides, you said you wanted to be early. It's five thirty. Shop opens at eight." My aunt blew out of the room as quickly as she'd breezed in.

Of course we're alive. People don't get killed in Mountain Shadows. We don't have crime. Well, burglaries, petty stuff. Most people don't even lock their doors. But then again, most people don't find diamonds buried in their yard, either. I'd have to speak with Uncle Roy about stricter security around here.

Opening Day! The thought spurred me to action. I threw aside the blankets and sprang from bed.

I'd already chosen the first day's outfit with great care, wanting to look the part of a candy store owner, not that I knew firsthand what that looked like. I could only imagine, which for me could be dangerous.

My red apron would look fabulous over the black dress with red pinstripes. And I hoped the black would help hide any spots of splattered chocolate. I ran my fingers over the cotton fabric as I passed the dress on my way to the shower.

Thirty minutes later, I leaned against the kitchen counter, sipping strong coffee. Aunt Eunice bustled around the kitchen as happy as a bee in a flower garden. I rubbed my sleep-deprived eyes. "Why are you so cheerful in the morning?"

"I wasn't the one chasing intruders around the house in the middle of the night." Aunt Eunice took the half-empty mug from my hands. "No more time. We've got to go."

"Two hours early isn't what I meant."

"We'll find plenty to occupy ourselves. And, by the way, I asked that nice girl from the town paper to come a little early to interview you."

"What girl, and how early?" A full-scale circus parade of nerves had started in my stomach, complete with elephants.

"Mabel Coffman. I told her seven."

"Seven! Mabel? She isn't a girl. She's got to be at least sixty years old."

"Wait awhile, and sixty won't seem so old to you. Today's sixty ain't like it used to be. I personally don't consider myself old."

Aunt Eunice shoved my purse into my hands. "She just turned fifty. Mabel's wrinkled from all the time she spends in her garden. I've told her to wear a hat, but that woman doesn't listen. She can't come at eight when the doors open 'cause she's a busy woman. She works at the paper part-time as a reporter and part-time as the receptionist. Somebody else will drop by later to take pictures."

I rolled my eyes and pushed open the screen door. "A new store is a big deal in this town. Couldn't they have sent somebody else?"

"Guess it ain't as important to other folks as you'd like it to be."

Ouch. That hurt. I stalked down the porch steps. Every single citizen in this town should be excited.

Aunt Eunice's truck sat in the driveway like some massive beast. Great. With all that had happened yesterday, I never did get my car from the church parking lot. Now I'd be stuck riding in my aunt's ancient candy-apple red pickup.

We bounced our way out of the driveway and shuddered toward the state highway. The truck whined each time Aunt Eunice shifted gears. A headache nagged at the base of my skull.

My spirits lifted as we turned onto Main Street. Summer Confections nestled between the post office and a general store. A few doors down sat my favorite place to while away the time: Grandma's Story Corner. The scrubbed front window of Summer Confections caught the morning sun, reflecting light into my eyes, and tears welled as I caught my first glance of the store's new sign.

I'd done it. I'd finally achieved my dream.

Aunt Eunice reached over and patted my knee. "It is a purty sight. Especially inside with all that wood and brass. You did good, sweetie."

I glanced down at my aunt's hand, crisscrossed with raised veins, and returned the pat. She'd nurtured and loved me for many years after the death of my parents, and the woman meant the world to me. "I couldn't have done it without you. I owe you a lot, Aunt Eunice."

"Oh, go on." She removed her hand, placing it back on the wheel, and steered the truck down the alley behind the store. But I noticed that her eyes glimmered.

I opened the door with my trembling hand and heaved against its weight. I moved slowly, taking a deep breath against the *rat-a-tat-tat* in my chest. Another deep breath, and I stepped inside.

The warm scent of chocolate greeted me, and I let my gaze travel over the shelves of pristine white boxes tied with gold ribbon. I stepped to the glass counter that displayed over fifty types of hand-dipped chocolates and trailed my fingers across the top. All mine. Every delectable bite. *Thank You, God, for making this possible.*

I straightened the already neat pile of brochures and checked the display in the window. Everything looked just as I wanted. I grinned at Aunt Eunice.

The back door opened, and a slightly rounded, red-faced woman barged in. A large leather satchel hung from one elbow. "Summer! Eunice! What a grand day!"

"It promises to be." Still grinning, I stepped forward to welcome the first person to my store. The woman pushed past me, hardly seeming to notice my proffered hand. If I hadn't jumped out of the way, she would've knocked me over.

Mabel Coffman plopped her satchel on the five-hundred-pound slab of marble and proceeded to rummage through her massive bag until she pulled out a tape recorder. I followed and gnawed my lower lip while scanning the slab for scratches.

"Okay. Now, I heard through the grapevine, mind you, that the two of you had a mighty big surprise on your property yesterday." The woman's eyes bugged from behind her wire-rimmed eyeglasses.

"Okay. Now," Aunt Eunice mocked, "are you here to talk about what we found or the opening of this store?"

Mabel shrugged. "Thought I could kill two birds with one stone."

I cringed, wishing she hadn't used the word *killed*. I looked her in the eye. "We should stick to the store. Confidentiality, you know."

"Oh sure." The other woman waved a hand. "Whatever. How many varieties of candy do you make?"

"Over fifty. All hand-dipped to per—"

"Chocolate?"

I frowned at the interruption. "Milk, dark, and white. Although white really isn't—"

"How much cash was there? Diamonds?"

"Excuse me?" Obviously, Mabel wasn't interested in the store.

Aunt Eunice slapped a palm flat on the marble slab. The sound reminded me of Uncle Roy slapping freshly gutted fish against the cutting board. "That's enough, Mabel. We ain't gonna tell you nothing about yesterday. You want to interview Summer about the store or not? 'Cause we got work to do."

"I don't know when you got to be such a spoilsport, Eunice." The woman's lips disappeared into a thin red line. "Joe down at the station won't give me any news, either. The public deserves to know what's going on. And it's my job to let them know."

"There isn't anything going on. If Joe didn't tell you, then who did?"

"Ladies." I held up my hands, hoping to prevent the verbal screaming match I knew to be inevitable. "It doesn't matter. It really doesn't."

The back door opened again, causing me to turn. Across the room, a woman so tiny a strong puff of wind could blow her over entered the store. A large camera hung from a strap around her neck, and she tilted slightly forward. Her thin face sported a freshly sunburned nose.

Mabel jumped to her feet. "Ruby Colville!"

Ruby's eyes narrowed. "Eunice, you said she'd be gone by the time I got here."

"She's early." Aunt Eunice plopped into the chair Mabel had vacated.

A feeling of helplessness rose in me as Mountain Shadows' most infamous enemies faced off. Five years ago, the two fancied the same widower, each hoping to win his affections over the other. Instead, the man disappeared with a woman half his age. Nevertheless, the two had never gotten over their bitter rivalry, despite both working at the local paper.

"Don't you have some flowers to photograph?" Mabel crossed her arms over her less-than-ample chest. "Vegetables to plant?" Ruby had won the blue ribbon three years running for her canned vegetables. Another thorn in Mabel's side.

"Don't you have some *almost* news to dig up?" Ruby's near-nonexistent eyebrows rose to an impossible height.

My perfect day was spiraling downhill. I cast a look of hopelessness at my aunt.

"That's enough!" Aunt Eunice stepped between the sparring women. "Mabel, you can get your interview later. Over the phone. Ruby, start snapping pictures of Summer then wait in the back room until people start arriving. Take a couple more pictures with the customers and then vanish."

"Oh, very well." Ruby motioned for me to stand behind the counter. "Smile like you just sold a five-pound box of chocolates."

I took a deep breath to calm myself, and Ruby snapped the picture. The woman stuck her lens cap back on the camera. Great. I probably looked like an inflated balloon. The morning sun shining through the window bounced off her diamond ring. The thing looked as large as a tennis ball.

"Wait. I wasn't ready." I reached out a hand to stop her.

"Not my problem, dearie. I told you I was taking the picture."

"But—" I stared in astonishment. Nothing about the morning seemed to be going as planned.

"Okay, I'll take another one." With great drama and heavy sighs, Ruby pulled off the lens cap and lifted the camera to her eye. "On the count of three. Pay attention now. One, two, three." She clicked the camera.

"Thank you." I smoothed my apron and stepped from behind the counter. One glance at the clock sent me scurrying into the back room. Seven forty-five! "Aunt Eunice, we've got to get some candy on. The store needs to smell like we actually make chocolate here."

"We do."

"You know what I mean." I plugged in the dipping machine. "Toss some milk chocolate in the dipper. I'm going to raise the blinds."

The sight beyond the window brought tears to my eyes. People stood shoulder to shoulder, pressing against the glass. Several smiled and waved as the blinds went up. When I unlocked the door fifteen minutes later, the crowd cheered. My hometown had come out to support me.

"Ethan!"

The object of my affections strolled into the store in the midst of the crowd, looking like he'd stepped out of a magazine. A casual magazine, since he was wearing jeans and a T-shirt, but definitely a magazine. I wanted nothing more than to run over and welcome him properly.

"I thought you couldn't make it." I leaned in closer. A flash exploded from Ruby's camera. Then she turned and left. I blinked against the colored dots. Why wouldn't the woman get a digital camera?

"I managed to get away for a few minutes." Ethan's gaze followed Ruby out of the store. "That's it? One picture?"

I shrugged. "I guess. People are acting very strange this morning." I reached for a prepacked one-pound box of candy. "Can I talk to you later?"

"Sure. I'll look around a bit. Maybe buy some candy for my sister."

He came! The man came! My heart did flips. The sight of Ethan meandering through the store distracted me, and instead of charging the customer eleven dollars, I rang up one hundred and eleven. "Oops." My fingers flew across the register keys, correcting the mistake.

"Summer!" Ethan's sister breezed in. "I have news!"

"April, Summer's busy."

"It'll only take a minute." April turned to Aunt Eunice. "Can you take over the register?"

"What are you girls up to now?" Aunt Eunice took her place behind the counter, leaving a half-packed box of candy on the counter.

"Girl stuff. Hi, Ethan."

He lifted a hand in greeting. April grabbed my arm and dragged me to the back room.

"What can be this important?" I pulled free of her grasp. "Did you see the line out there? It's my opening day."

"I was listening to the police scanner, and there's a man missing. I thought you'd want to know."

"Missing?"

April's face lit up. "Since day before yesterday."

"You seem happy."

"No, just wound up." She stepped closer and lowered her voice. "What if it's his blood on the glove?"

My mind shifted into overdrive. My suspicions of a possible murder grew stronger. Why else hide a bloody glove? "Who is he?"

"Richard Bland. Diamond broker."

"Diamond broker? What's a diamond broker doing in Mountain Shadows? The jewelry store maybe?" The line of customers in front of Aunt Eunice now stood three people deep. "Look, April. Come to my house later. You can tell me everything."

April's body trembled with apparent excitement. "Okay. I'll be there before Ethan gets home. He's got a meeting. He'll try to stop me otherwise." She gave me a quick hug. "I feel like, like, you know—that famous English detective. Sherlock Christie, or something."

"It's Agatha Christie. She's the author," I called after her. "Her character was Miss Marple." I took my aunt's place packing boxes as my mind mulled over what April had said. I couldn't fathom how I'd make it through the rest of the day without knowing all the facts.

"What did my sister want?" Ethan leaned on the counter. His blue eyes bored into mine.

"Uh, nothing?"

"Summer." Ethan scowled. "Please tell me you aren't getting my sister involved in your gumshoeing."

"I'm not getting her involved in anything."

I ducked my head and reached for a container of vanilla creams. Well, I wasn't. She did this willingly, so I wasn't lying. A recent lesson from church nagged at my mind. The message mentioned God seeing things in black-and-white. Right and wrong. I pushed the thought aside. God wouldn't let my misgiving alone. He tickled at the recesses of my mind. Guilt rose in me.

"I don't believe you. A white lie is still a lie." He straightened and looked around the store. "Quite a turnout. Can you pack me a one-pound box?"

I forced a grin. My lips trembled. "Sure. Isn't it wonderful? I just hope Aunt Eunice and I made enough candy. Ethan, I'm—" A customer edged between him and the counter.

Reaching around the woman, Ethan paid for his box. "If not, they'll have to come back. See you later, Summer." He flashed me his killer smile with those to-die-for dimples, and I leaned against the counter for support.

Before I had the opportunity to apologize and admit to my falsehood, Ethan left. My gaze followed him to the door.

"Summer, I need a box wrapped." My aunt's request broke into my thoughts.

With one more glance to where Ethan had disappeared, I made my way to the wrapping counter. A roll of thick white paper with gold swirls sat next to gold and white curling ribbon. Three boxes sat waiting for my wrapping skills. One three-pound box and two one-pounders. I found myself calculating the day's profits in my head.

April leaned against her car when I pulled into my driveway. In spite of Ethan's teasing about her car looking like a gangster ride, she'd tinted the windows as dark as legally possible. I smiled at her reasoning. Said it would help to prevent sun damage to her delicate skin. She pointed at her watch and mouthed the words, "You're late."

After cutting the car's engine, I pushed open the door. "Sorry. We don't close the store until five. People still wanted to buy chocolate. One man bought a whole slab for his girlfriend. That's fifty pounds!" I grabbed my purse and used my hip to close the door. "I should've had you meet me at the Coffee Barn. I'm running on empty."

"Got it." April leaned through her car's open window and retrieved a cardboard carrier with two frozen mocha coffee drinks.

"You're the best." I quickened my pace. "Let's head to my room. Aunt Eunice will be home soon, and I don't want her eavesdropping."

"Maybe she can help. She knows everyone around here." April handed me a coffee.

"No. Well, maybe." I unlocked the front door. "I don't know whether I want her involved or not. What if things get dangerous?"

April giggled. "Then I'm not sure I want to be involved."

"Come on. Don't be a ninny." I led the way. The two of us plopped across the bed, and I kicked off my shoes.

"Did you hear about our intruder last night?" I asked before dragging hard on my straw.

"No." April's eyes widened. "Tell."

I recounted last night's events with as much drama as I could.

"Weren't you afraid? I would've been." April leaned back. "If someone broke into my house, I'd be hiding in the closet."

"I was afraid afterward. During, I was excited." I leaned closer to April. "And it showed me I'm on to something." I held up a finger. "One, why did someone choose my yard to stash the diamonds? Two"—another finger went up—"why take the time to break into my house, knowing the diamonds and cash probably weren't here?"

"Don't forget the bloody glove."

"Right. And three, has someone met with foul play?" I rolled over on my back, holding my drink high to prevent spilling it. "Four—or maybe it's actually part of three—we have a missing diamond broker. Related? Plus, I found footprints. Small prints, but bigger than mine, and not very deep."

"If your Midnight Blue hadn't died, we'd know nothing about any of this." April slurped her drink. "I tried telling Ethan it means we're supposed to check into this case. He keeps telling me to leave it to Joe. Who, by the way, is looking particularly fine. Anyway, Ethan would have a conniption fit if he knew we were thinking about digging deeper."

My heart leaped at the mention of Ethan's name. "It'd be great if he'd solve this with us."

April sat up. "No, it wouldn't. He'd tell us what to do."

"You're only saying that because he's your brother.

Admit it, April. If he wasn't your brother, you'd think he was hot." I looked at my friend. "Do you realize we haven't done this in ages? Hanging out and talking? Getting older really stinks."

"We're not that old. Not quite thirty. But it is fun. I've got to be getting home. Let me know if you hear anything." She lowered her voice. "Or want to go on a stakeout."

I grabbed a pillow and tossed it at her. "Get out of here."

April bounced from the room, leaving me to my musings. I rested the drink on my stomach. Who should I put on my list of suspects? My mind set itself on the bloody glove. *Blue with red flowers. A woman's glove?* Mabel gardened in her spare time. So did Ruby Colville. And so did half the population of Mountain Shadows. I sighed.

Was there anyone new in town? I'd have to ask Uncle Roy whether he'd had any unfamiliar customers. Maybe I could talk Ethan into taking me to the dance at the community center on Friday night. They were throwing a ballroom dancing night. It'd be fun, plus just about everyone would be there.

Closing my eyes, I imagined myself floating around the floor in Ethan's arms. How would I convince him to go? Could I talk him into going as my protector? Play the helpless female? A smile spread across my face. It might work.

He'd think me an idiot. I slammed my hands on the mattress. The drink tilted, dumping an icy river of chocolate coffee down my side. I screamed and bolted to my feet.

Footsteps pounded up the stairs. A second later, the man of my dreams barged into the room, worry etched across his face. "Summer?"

With outstretched hands, I stood and stared aghast into his face. "I spilled my drink."

Ethan leaned against the door frame and laughed. "Good thing you're wearing black." He glanced toward the bed. "Were you drinking lying down?"

I pushed past him, choosing not to answer. "What are you doing here anyway? And why are you in my room?" *Horror.* A glance over my shoulder showed the brown stain across my bed. I glared at Ethan then grabbed his arm to pull him into the hallway.

"I heard you scream." He grinned down at me, melting my heart. "Am I your knight in shining armor?"

If you only knew. "Of course not. I don't need a knight coming to rescue me. I'm a woman of the millennium." *Oh, but I do need you.* I released his arm and stepped back as if stung.

"Okay, then. Will you do me the honor of going to the dance with me?"

My mouth gaped open. How'd he know? My traitorous face heated. Had he guessed my feelings for him? "It's formal."

Humor shone in his eyes. "I know. I'm not afraid of dressing like a penguin. Is that a yes?"

Struggling to appear nonchalant, while inside I danced the salsa, I shrugged. "Yes. No one else has asked me."

His smile faded, despite the continuing sparkle in his eyes, and I could've kicked myself. "Great. I'll pick you up at six for dinner. April's coming with us."

"I need to tell you something." Now seemed as good

a time as any to tell him about my falsehood.

"Later. When I pick you up."

I clapped a hand to my forehead as Ethan made his way down the stairs. No one else had asked me? I groaned. *It's official. I'm a dunce.*

Standing at the top of the stairs, I stared down the carpet runner as Ethan banged out the front door, the screen swinging shut behind him. Seconds later, Aunt Eunice bustled in, her face flushed from exertion.

"Girl, there's been a murder."

5

W hat?" I was full of interesting responses this evening.

Grasping the railing, Aunt Eunice pulled herself up the stairs. She puffed like a winded racehorse and, wheezing, balanced her hands. "Some stranger. Gone. Dead."

"Richard Bland. A diamond broker. April told me. They find his body?"

Aunt Eunice shook her head. "I don't know who you're talking about. Never heard of a Bland. No, this young fellow visited the Ruperts. Name was David Young. Po-lice said he'd been dead since late Tuesday night or the early hours of Wednesday."

My aunt straightened and clutched her chest. "I ran all the way from the mailbox to tell you. Probably going to have a heart attack."

She would've had to run about thirty feet. "How'd you find out?" I took Aunt Eunice's arm and helped her down the stairs to the kitchen. I flicked on the light against the growing dusk.

"Mabel stopped by when I was checking the mail. Seems she heard it on the po-lice scanner." Aunt Eunice collapsed into a chair. "The young man was visiting the youngest Rupert. Terri Lee, I think. Anyway, they found him buried in the woods outside of town. Some dog dug him up."

Terri Lee's back in town? I shuddered, refusing to think of my high school nemesis. Leaving my aunt to recuperate, I pulled open a drawer and rummaged for a pencil. "Aunt Eunice, where's paper? I need to make a list."

"Same place it's always been, Summer."

"Oh." I snatched a small spiral notebook from the drawer next to the refrigerator and rushed to the table. I'd have to get my own supplies if I planned to solve this case.

"What are you writing?" Aunt Eunice leaned her elbows on the white-speckled Formica in front of her. The red in her face subsided, and her breathing returned to normal.

"A suspect list." I tapped the pencil on the table. "Did you know we have a missing diamond broker?"

"I do now." She pointed at my pad of paper. "List him."

I wrote RICHARD BLAND and then gnawed the eraser as my mind ran through the names of Mountain Shadows' residents. I knew I'd find a lot of suspicious characters at the dance tomorrow night. I added Mabel and Ruby.

"Why'd you put them there?" My aunt scowled at me. "They wouldn't hurt anyone but each other."

"I noticed the rock on Ruby's finger this morning and heard through the grapevine that Mabel is driving around town in a brand-new Caddy."

"So?"

"Where'd they get the money? You said yourself they only work part-time." I rose from my chair and paced. "I'm writing down the Ruperts, too, since it's their guest who's turned up dead." My stomach lurched at the thought of an actual body.

Aunt Eunice stood and planted herself in front of me. "Then you might as well put me down, too. You've got all my friends." She reminded me of a short, round bull terrier. A cute one, but if she let out a bark, I'd be out of there.

"Aunt Eunice." She whirled and stalked past my outstretched hand. "I didn't mean—" I dropped my hand and returned to my list.

My aunt poked her head around the corner long enough to scream at me, "You might want to take a minute and ask God who should go on that list!" Heavy footsteps signaled her march up the stairs.

Great. Now there were two things I needed to speak with God about. My lie being first. Most of my Christian life, my aunt, Ethan, or April has told me to think and ask God before acting.

Summer, did you pray about it? Don't be so impulsive. Did you ask God first? All my life, people have told me to wait on God. Why is it so hard for me to give the control of my life over to Him? I would have to have a serious conversation with Him during my next devotion time. I'd need to remember to pray for guidance and wisdom. And not to do something stupid.

"What about dinner?" I yelled.

"Not hungry!" Aunt Eunice called down.

That didn't go well, and my stomach growled. I opened the refrigerator and stared into the food-packed recesses. My aunt, the queen of stockpiling. If she didn't visit the grocery store for a month, we still wouldn't go hungry. It didn't take long for me to pull out the makings for a meal.

I soon sat back at the table with a cold diet cola and

a sandwich. I frowned and took a bite of my ham and Swiss dinner.

It didn't look like I'd be getting much help from Aunt Eunice. I really hadn't been aware she had such a tight friendship with Mabel and Ruby. Shrugging, I took another bite. Counting the Ruperts, I had six suspects. I'd need to do some in-depth detective work tomorrow night.

Truly growled and bounded for the kitchen door. She scratched at it and let out a bark. The hair on my neck rose, and my skin prickled. I got to my feet and whipped around to stare out the window. The wind had increased, blowing dirt and small debris across the yard, but I couldn't see a reason for the dog's fuss. Tree branches slapped at the darkening sky. Thick clouds turned the early evening almost dark.

I reached for the door handle then stopped, remembering all the silly B horror movies where the heroine walks straight into danger. I withdrew my hand and wished Aunt Eunice hadn't gone upstairs. Maybe it was Uncle Roy returning from the nursery. I shook my head. I hadn't heard the rumble of his truck coming into the driveway.

"Truly. Come." I inched my way from the kitchen and into the hall then bounded up the stairs. "Aunt Eunice!"

She shrieked as I burst into her room. "Land sakes, child! Are you trying to kill me? You know storms make me nervous."

"There's someone outside." I parted the curtains and peered out. "Call 911."

"Did you lock the front door?" Aunt Eunice sat up

from where she'd been lounging against her bed pillows.

"No. Didn't you?"

"I was busy telling you about that missing boy." She clutched a pillow to her chest. "Besides, it wasn't dark then. Go on."

My heart leaped into my throat. "What?"

"You'll have to lock the door, Summer."

"Can't I just stay in here with you?" Going downstairs alone did not give me a warm, fuzzy feeling. "We could lock ourselves in."

"There's no phone. Do you have your cell phone?"

"Downstairs." I glanced around for something to use as a weapon and grabbed one of Aunt Eunice's mud boots. "Okay. If I'm not back in five—"

"Good grief, Summer. What do you plan on doing with that boot?"

"Throw it at anyone who jumps out at me. Cause a distraction." Nervous giggles escaped. "I didn't see anything else."

Aunt Eunice nodded. "Good luck."

I nudged the dog aside with my foot and left her with Aunt Eunice. Never did the hall seem to stretch so far or appear so dark. Clichés from a half-dozen slash-and-gore movies ran through my mind. *This is real, Summer.* I clutched the boot tight against me.

I worked my way downstairs, my heart beating in time with each step. Tree branches scraped against the house, and I froze. Not hearing anything else, I kept going. Now would be a good time to pray.

Lightning flashed, thunder rolled, and the lights went out. Stifling a scream, I plastered myself against the wall. "God, keep me safe. Please."

I scooted to the living room.

Footsteps pounded from the front porch.

I rushed forward.

Threw the dead bolt on the door.

Then the chain.

The knob turned.

I fled to the kitchen. Where was Uncle Roy and his trusty gun when you needed them? Did he really have to work late at the nursery unloading the pallet of fertilizer? "Now I lay me down to sleep—" *No, definitely not that prayer. Wait. They changed the words.* How did it go now? *Never mind. Something else.* "Our Father, who art in heaven—"

Lightning skittered across the sky again. In the brief flash, I spotted the outline of a figure. The back door!

I ran through the dark kitchen yelping with pain when my foot slammed into the leg of a chair. I slipped and landed with a thump on my backside. The door creaked open. I aimed as a head appeared around the door frame.

"Summer!"

"Ethan?" He caught the boot in one hand.

I struggled to my feet and limped into his arms. "Someone's outside."

"I know. I came back to get my house keys. I think I left them on the foyer table." He untangled my arms from around his neck and pushed inside. "When I pulled up, someone jumped from the front porch and disappeared into the woods behind the house. I tried following but lost sight of him." He held me at arm's length. "Are you all right? Where's Eunice and Roy?"

"I'm fine. Aunt Eunice is upstairs, hiding beneath

the covers. Uncle Roy hasn't returned from work. I told my aunt to call the police." I slumped into a kitchen chair. "So, it wasn't my imagination."

"No, Summer, it wasn't." Ethan parted the curtains and peered out. "Your uncle told me about last night. Someone is looking for something, and I don't want you in the way."

Looking for what? More diamonds? My heart lodged in my throat.

"What have you stirred up?" Ethan turned and crossed his arms.

"Nothing. I haven't even spoken to anyone yet." Despite my having won the prize for being a scaredy-cat, I couldn't help but be intrigued. I'd definitely be digging beneath some rosebushes tomorrow.

The silky softness of the chocolate invited my fingers to linger. I tested the temperature. Pouring the melted dark liquid onto the chilled marble relaxed me. Lazy letters swirled through the chocolate as I worked. Enough. Daydreaming wouldn't put candy on the counter.

I lined the dark cups for nut clusters in neat rows, mixed the crushed cashews with the cooled candy, then allowed my mind to return to its wandering. The events of the past couple of days ran through my mind the same way my fingers moved through the chocolate.

"You seem miles away." Aunt Eunice dropped an unmelted chunk of chocolate into the pot sitting in front of me.

"What could the prowler be looking for? Joe has the

diamonds and the cash." I'd so wanted to stay home and do some hunting.

Aunt Eunice shrugged. "Don't come in tomorrow. I can handle things here. You go search around." She smiled and winked. "And don't worry about a thing tonight on your big date."

"It's not a date." I wanted to strangle April the next time I saw her. If she had twisted Ethan's arm in order for him to ask me to the dance, I'd be mortified. A mischievous plot formed in my head. Surely April had convinced Ethan to ask me. Now I'd get Joe to take her. I knew she had a new dress. She'd planned to tag along with me and her brother.

"I can investigate after work." I scraped the now lumpy, cooled mix from my hands. "Would you unlock the door and let the customers in? I need to make a phone call."

Aunt Eunice would probably lecture me on staying out of other people's business if she knew what I planned, so I ducked into the restroom and dialed my cell phone.

"Joe? It's me."

"Hello." A yawn followed.

"Did I wake you?" I glanced at my watch. Eight thirty. Definitely time for him to be up.

"Yes. I worked late last night, and I'm not scheduled for today. What do you want?"

"Do you have a date for the ball tonight?" I chewed the cuticle of my thumb.

"No, why? You want to go with me?"

"No. *Eww.* We're cousins. And not kissing cousins. I happen to know someone who's dying for you to take her."

"Who?" His voice perked up.

"April Banning."

"April? Wants to go with me? I don't know, Summer. I can't dance. Especially fancy twirling."

"She can teach you. It'd be better than her going alone. And, so far, that's her only option."

"So you're telling me I'm better than nothing."

"Well, yeah." Duh. "Will you take her or not?"

"Sure. What time do I pick her up?"

"Seven forty-five. At my house. We're getting ready together. And, Joe, our prowler visited again last night." I braced myself for what would come next.

"What? Why didn't anyone call me?"

"I told Aunt Eunice to call you, but she wouldn't leave her bedroom. I meant to later, after I got downstairs, but Ethan showed up. He scared them off. Have you been able to find out anything about the diamonds?"

Joe's sigh vibrated through the phone. "Nothing. No fingerprints. No filed reports. Nothing. And, if I did know anything, it'd be classified."

"Hmm. Okay. Gotta go. Chocolate is waiting. See you tonight."

I pushed the button to disconnect the call and leaned against the toilet tank. Obviously, I couldn't rely on the police to find out anything. If I didn't solve the case, who would?

I pushed the door open and rejoined my aunt who looked at me in obvious puzzlement. Giving her a sheepish smile, I slid my cell phone into my pocket. I could feel her eyes burning into my back as I washed my hands.

"What's on your mind, Aunt Eunice?"

"Do you always take the phone into the bathroom?"

"The police don't have any clues on who buried the diamonds or who's been skulking around the house." I turned, drying my hands on a white cotton towel.

"And you plan on solving it for them?"

I resumed my perch on the stool. I could do it. I grew up on Agatha Christie and Nancy Drew and avidly read today's mystery writers. All I had to do was follow the clues, right? "Aren't you curious?"

"Yes. But not enough to make Roy angry with me. You shouldn't, either. This person could be dangerous." She lifted the filled tray of cashew clusters and walked to the refrigerator.

"I'll be careful."

"Right." Aunt Eunice snorted.

⁓

"You look beautiful," I told April. She stood clothed in a sherbet pink gown that floated around her ankles as she moved.

The two of us made a pretty picture, and I smiled. My sky blue dress with a tight bodice and layers of sheer gauze flowed to midcalf. I looked like a princess. Aunt Eunice had outdone herself when she made our ball gowns. We both wore our hair in French twists and kept the makeup subtle. I wanted Ethan to see me. Not my makeup.

The doorbell rang, and Aunt Eunice yelled for us to hurry. I smirked at April's reflection. "By the way, you're going to the dance with Joe. He's picking you up here." I spun, twirling my dress, and headed downstairs.

"What? Wait!" April ran after me. Catching hold

of my arm, she whirled me around. "Stop. What're you talking about? What do you mean Joe's taking me to the dance?"

"You like him, don't you?"

"Well, yeah, but—"

"You had Ethan ask me, and I set you up with Joe. Now we're even." I pulled my arm free.

"Summer, I didn't tell Ethan to ask you. He did that himself." She shook her head and brushed past, leaving me feeling like an idiot.

Ethan and Joe stood at the bottom of the stairs, corsages in hand, looking absolutely divine in navy suits. Of course, my blond knight looked the best. April hadn't coerced Ethan to invite me. Could he possibly have romantic feelings toward me? I floated down the stairs. I doubt my stilettos touched the carpet runner.

"Pick Joe's brain about the case once he's relaxed," I whispered in April's ear. She nodded and linked her arm with the red-faced, off-duty police officer.

Ethan slid from the car and opened the door for me. Tucking my hand through my date's proffered arm, I felt odd, like a girl going to the prom. Like a nervous sixteen-year-old the high school quarterback asked to the dance.

Holding the door wide, Ethan ushered me inside the dimly lit hall where dancers whirled and twirled across a parquet floor. April and I handed our purses to an elderly man designated as the coat-check person.

The community center glowed with clear twinkle

lights both inside and out. They'd polished the wooden floor to a high sheen, and women glided by in gowns of every imaginable color. Since a professional dancer had moved to Mountain Shadows and taught ballroom dancing, a summer ball had become a much-anticipated annual event. Excitement surged through the air with laughter and music.

After a couple of promenades, I remembered why we were there. I scanned the room so often my hair threatened to come loose from its pins. Everyone seemed to be enjoying themselves. No one appeared threatening. I chewed the inside of my lip.

Who is that couple? What about that man over there? Or the woman serving cake?

"I'm right here, Summer."

"Huh?"

"Me. Ethan Banning. Your date. Your attention is everywhere but where it should be, and even I know that during the fox-trot you're supposed to be smiling over my right shoulder."

My face grew warm. "I'm trying to see who all's here."

Since he wanted my attention, now would be the perfect time to apologize for lying to him. *God, give me the words, please.* "Ethan, the other day at the store, I—"

A woman so beautiful and so artificial-looking that I automatically disliked her glided into the room. Her scarlet gown caught the twinkling lights like flames. Her raven hair hung down her back, brushing to where the low-cut gown stopped.

I suddenly felt like I was back in high school, competing against Terri Lee for homecoming queen. I'd lost and childishly still nursed a grudge. I hadn't forgiven her for telling the principal she'd seen me passed out at an after-game party. She'd gone so far as to blackmail witnesses into backing up her story. I'd withdrawn from the competition in shame, not bothering to clear my name.

Glancing up, I noticed Ethan's wide-eyed stare and promptly swerved us away from her.

"I'm supposed to lead, Summer."

"Oh. Right." I swiveled to see. Where had the vampiress disappeared to? *Great.* She glided in our direction.

"Ethan Banning?" Her voice poured over us like melted butter, complete with a soft Southern drawl. Nothing nasal about this woman.

"Terri Lee?" Ethan stopped, dropping his hand from my waist. "You've grown up."

"Yes, I have." Suddenly, her eyes were on me. "How are you, Summer? Living the dream?" Her lips turned up a smirk.

"Yes, actually. I own Summer Confections. The place to buy the finest handmade chocolates." I kept my hand tight on Ethan's arm. *Forgive me for being catty, Lord, but I'm not going to beat this woman in the looks department.*

"Ah, an entrepreneur. How mahvelous." And with those words, she dismissed me and turned her black eyes to Ethan.

"What are you doing back in town, Terri Lee?"

"Working at Shadow Jewelers. I'm a designer now. They've got quite a few of my pieces featured."

Well, la-dee-da. I designed things, too. Mouthwatering chocolates. Nothing made a person feel better than great chocolate. Not even diamonds. Who said they were a girl's best friend? Give me a vanilla cream any day. I stepped between Ethan and the evil fire-temptress. "I'm thirsty, Ethan. Would you mind getting me a drink?"

He frowned but nodded. I turned back to Mountain Shadows' most dangerous. "How long do you plan on staying in town, Terri Lee?"

She patted her date, Duane Parker of all people, sending him off after Ethan. The man nodded, looking uncomfortable in an ill-fitting tux, and left to do her bidding. Terri Lee's gaze flicked to the returning Ethan, and my heart plummeted to the depths of my stomach.

"Forever, 'cause I've come home. And I'm looking forward to reconnecting with old acquaintances."

"Beginning with Duane?" I should've bit my tongue.

Her eyes shot daggers. "Yes, Duane. For starters. We dated in high school. Turns out he knows a thing or two about gemstones. He read a lot while in prison and can be quite useful to me. Don't you think?

I sat at the candy-dipping machine the next morning, forlorn, using my finger to swirl the chocolate into cursive letters on top of the covered vanilla creams. I hadn't gathered any evidence on the diamond case while at the ball. Worse, Ethan hadn't kissed me good night at the door. Instead, he'd chucked me under the chin like a two-year-old. I bet he would've kissed Terri Lee. Kissed her so hard the red would've melted off her dress.

On the way home, April and Joe had chattered like a couple of magpies. Apparently, their date had gone as planned. I hoped she'd at least remembered to garner information from him.

I sighed. There had to be a better way of gathering clues. Watching people didn't work. I'd bet my last dollar the guilty party was Terri Lee. She was too beautiful to be innocent. I sighed again.

"What's wrong with you this morning? You should've stayed home like I told you to if all you're going to do is mope around." Aunt Eunice removed the full tray and replaced it with one I had to complete. Strawberry creams this time.

"Do you mind if I take off for a bit? I'd like to run by the bookstore."

"Didn't I just say that? Why is this business with the diamonds so important to you, Summer?" She planted her fists on hips covered with a red apron. "Why do you feel compelled to get involved?"

Why did I? Maybe I wanted people to stop thinking

of me as an empty-headed Barbie doll. I didn't look like a Barbie doll, not having the proportions that famous female possessed. All my life, I'd been sheltered. Protected. I wanted everyone to know I could take care of myself. That I was stronger than my thin, five-foot-two-inch frame suggested.

"Just for fun." I ran the last cream through the machine and flipped the OFF switch. "Keeps my brain functioning."

"Keeps your brain functioning, my foot. A girl your age doesn't have to worry about a brain going lax. Not yet." The bell over the front door tinkled, and Aunt Eunice went to wait on the customer, muttering under her breath.

Two doors down from Summer Confections sat the greatest bookstore in the world: Grandma's Story Corner. They'd expanded the store over the years, as folks from neighboring towns came to Mountain Shadows for the Story Corner's ambience. Grandma sold freshly baked pastries and delicious fragrant coffee served hot or frozen. And if Grandma didn't carry what you wanted, she could get it for you.

I pushed open the dark walnut door and took a big sniff. I loved the smell of new books. Had ever since I was a child. That welcome aroma drifted to me along with the smell of warm, yeasty pastries.

"Good morning, Summer." Grandma didn't look the stereotype. She was tall and thin with dyed, coal black hair, painted-on eyebrows, and heavily outlined lips. But the woman knew her business.

"Good morning, Grandma." I leaned on the counter, eyeing the blueberry muffins. "I'm looking for a book on crime solving. And I want a muffin and a frozen mocha."

"Are you going into the detective business?" Grandma lifted the muffin with a pair of silver-plated grips. She smiled a greeting at a couple who stood behind me.

"No, uh, I'm writing a novel." *Great. Now I'll have to write one.* I didn't want another lie on my conscience.

"Then I'd suggest the 'Dummy Corner.'" She pushed the button on the blender, mixing my coffee.

Dummy Corner? I was getting a complex.

"You can find a book on anything suited for the ordinary layperson."

"Okay. Thanks." I prayed no one would see me as I made my way to the back corner of the store, avoiding other patrons. I let out a breath of relief once I reached the section. A wide selection lined the walls, from *The Dolt's Complete Guide to Calculus* to *The Dolt's Complete Guide to Learning Spanish*. And right there, staring at me, *The Dolt's Complete Guide to Private Investigating.* I ran a finger down the table of contents. "What It Takes to Be a PI," "Becoming a PI," and so on. I completely forgot how offended I should be from the title.

Ecstatic, I rushed to Grandma and shoved the book into her hands. "I'll take it."

"I don't get many requests for books like this." She rang up my purchases, and I fished a twenty out of my purse. "Must be some novel you're writing."

"I hope so. A mystery." *And I'll title it* Summer Investigations.

I felt more like one of Charlie's angels than Miss Marple. "Could you put the book in a brown sack?" I wanted to keep my aunt from seeing what I bought.

When I returned, April sat behind the counter. Things were obviously slow at the real estate office where she worked as a receptionist. I stuffed the package, along with my purse, under the counter. No customers milled about, so I grabbed her arm and pulled her to the back room. "Find out anything from Joe last night?"

"Yes." She perched on one of the stools. "He's the sweetest guy."

"About the case, April."

"Oh, that." She waved a hand dismissively in the air. "A little, as in not much. Still no clues, no fingerprints, no DNA, nothing. But these things take time, I've heard. No one at the station can figure out who keeps breaking into your house or why they'd want to. The only newcomers, besides the missing broker, are Terri Lee Rupert and Duane Parker. I'm not sure they'd be considered newcomers, since they used to live here." April plucked a strawberry cream from a nearby tray. "Did you see Terri Lee last night?"

"Yes. I saw her." The green-eyed monster raised its ugly head. "Ethan couldn't keep his eyes off her."

April popped the candy in her mouth. "Well, they used to date, you know. Before he went to college."

"I'd chosen to forget that."

April wiped her hands on a nearby towel. "Thank you for setting me up with Joe. I had a wonderful time. We're going out again on his next night off." She hopped off the stool, gave me a quick hug, and headed out the door with a wave to Aunt Eunice.

At least someone had a wonderful time last night. I'd expected more from Ethan.

He'd even seemed preoccupied during the drive

home. Maybe as payback for my own preoccupation while dancing? Or the return of a long-lost love? The day's sunshine disappeared, casting my heart into shadow.

I spent my time making candy and let Aunt Eunice handle the customers. There weren't many. A few came in for gifts, and I'd look up to study their faces, hoping to spot a potential suspect. My fingers itched to turn the pages of my new book. By tomorrow I'd know everything about being a private investigator.

"We need more peanut brittle." Aunt Eunice handed the last bag to a waiting customer. "And someone requested cashew brittle. Do you know how to make that?"

"Same recipe. Just use cashews instead of peanuts." It looked like I'd be putting in longer hours restocking candy after all.

My cell phone rang a jaunty melody, and I wiped my hands on my apron before grabbing it. Caller ID said ETHAN BANNING. My breath caught, and my finger paused over the button. I experienced hope and fear at the same time. The music continued to play, and I sent a prayer for peace heavenward.

"Hi," I said.

"Hello, Summer. I called to let you know I had a good time last night."

"You did?" I leaned against the wall behind me, getting a warm and fuzzy feeling.

"Why do you sound so surprised?"

"I don't know. You seemed a bit preoccupied."

"And you didn't?"

"I'm sorry. You're right." I decided to switch the topic of conversation. "April and Joe seemed to get along real nice."

"Yeah, Joe's a great guy."

I gnawed the inside of my cheek for a moment. "And you met up with an old friend."

"Who? Terri Lee? Yeah, it's good to see her again."

Who was he kidding? "April said you two were close once upon a time." I studied the ragged cuticles on my right hand, trying to sound nonchalant, while inside, my heart galloped.

"A long time ago. Gotta go, Summer. Thanks again." *Click.*

I wasn't sure how to interpret the conversation. Could he be interested in Terri Lee? I'd decided to add a visit to the jewelers at the bottom of my growing list of things to do. Maybe I could get some feedback from the wonderful, beautiful Terri Lee. Was she interested in Ethan? I decided to make her number one on my list.

<hr />

I was on my way to church, still with no clue, literally, about where the diamonds came from. The as-of-yet-unopened *Dolt Guide* lay on my nightstand, and I vowed to spend my afternoon learning everything it had to offer.

I drove into the church parking lot, and the first thing I laid eyes on was Beauty Queen Terri Lee hanging on Ethan's arm. Well, maybe she wasn't hanging on him, but one dainty paw rested in the crook of his elbow. Why wasn't the man greeting parishioners? He did have a job to do.

The advice my aunt gave me about asking God who should go on my suspect list had me pause and offer a quick prayer before I exited the car. My eyes scanned the area for anyone God might bring to mind. I slammed my car door, took a step, and jerked to a stop. I'd shut the hem of my dress in the door, and wouldn't you know it, Ethan and Terri Lee stared in my direction.

Ethan shot me a huge, dimpled grin, while Terri Lee arched one finely tweezed brow. I gave the pair what I hoped to be a dainty wave and swept my full skirt free.

"Good morning, Summer." Ethan chuckled as I breezed past him.

"Good morning, Ethan. Terri Lee." I gripped my Bible tighter to my chest. "I enjoyed our phone conversation yesterday, Ethan. It really brightened my day." I gave Terri Lee a smile and entered the building.

As usual, I made a beeline for the coffee bar to purchase my drink. This time I pulled up a chair at one of the little café tables. Although I hated to admit one of my fellow churchgoers could be a criminal, I intended to scrutinize everyone.

Ethan and Terri Lee entered and went their separate ways. Terri Lee went toward the main sanctuary, and Ethan took his position to greet those arriving. He looked amazing. Tan Dockers and a black polo shirt set off the golden tone of his skin and hair, and I temporarily forgot what I searched for.

"Hey, Summer." April pulled up a chair across from me. "What are you doing?"

"I'm on a stakeout, kind of."

"Who are you staking out? My brother?" April turned to look.

"No. I'm people watching." I twirled my plastic cup in the condensation on the tabletop. "Maybe something will jump out at me. I'm clueless."

April giggled. "Everyone knows that."

"I mean about the case."

"Sounds like fun. I'll help." She crossed her legs then bolted upright like a jack-in-the box. "There's Joe. See you later."

So much for my sidekick. The first strums of praise music drifted from the sanctuary, and people stopped mingling to merge in one coursing wave toward their seats. One man stood alone. Tall, dark, and mysterious. Mysterious because all I'd seen of him before was the back of his head. Mister GQ had to be Nate, the new barista.

He stood a few inches shorter than Ethan's height with chestnut hair and mahogany eyes. I couldn't help but notice how handsome he was. Movie-star handsome— but I preferred my men golden. The man glanced around the atrium, caught my gaze, and headed into the men's restroom. I'd have to ask Aunt Eunice about him. She knew everyone in town, or at least about everyone in town.

I pitched my drink and went to find a seat. I had lingered at the coffee bar too long and had to sit near the rear of the sanctuary. Aunt Eunice waved for me to sit next to her. I took one look at the seat in the corner and shook my head. Another row up, I squeezed past a rather heavy-set woman, muttering apologies.

Two rows up, I spotted the back of Terri Lee's head. From that point on, worship was a struggle. She probably sang like an angel. I craned my neck to see whether the mystery man had made an appearance but couldn't spot him. I remained preoccupied during the announcements, not paying attention until the pastor spoke about trust. From Psalm 25, verses 2 and 3.

"In you I trust, O my God. Do not let me be put to shame, nor let my enemies triumph over me."

I sat higher in my seat. The pastor's words confirmed the raven-haired temptress wouldn't win Ethan. The day grew brighter.

"No one whose hope is in you will ever be put to shame, but they will be put to shame who are treacherous without excuse."

I wasn't treacherous, was I? I felt like the pastor singled me out. Was everyone staring at me? I squirmed in my seat and tried to refocus. My hope was in the Lord. Always had been, always would be. Somehow, I knew my crush on Ethan wasn't what the verse spoke of. I squirmed again.

Something hit me in the back of the head, and I looked to where my aunt sat. She wore a scowl on her face and shook her head as she pointed toward the front of the chair. The wadded paper wrapper from a straw lay on the empty seat next to me. How old did she think I was? She hadn't chastised me that way since childhood.

My face flamed. I'd been acting like a child. Not sitting still and paying attention to those around me instead of the pastor. *I'm sorry, Lord. I promise to do better.* And I did, keeping my eyes glued to the pulpit.

After church, an empty afternoon beckoned. Torn between digging up my yard, searching for whatever my night visitor had been looking for, or learning how to be a private investigator, the yard won. What if there were more diamonds buried beneath my roses?

Once home, I rushed upstairs, donned my blue

overalls with fuchsia-colored flowers, let the dog out, and then hurried to my garden. Perched on my pink kneepad, I dug beneath one bush after another.

Two hours later, I brushed a dirty forearm across a sweaty brow and stood to ease the kinks out of my back. I'd found nothing besides worms and roly-poly bugs. Not to mention the hassle Truly proved to be as she nosed around the holes and got in my way.

"Summer, what are you doing?" Ethan leaned against the house, ankles crossed and hands shoved into the pockets of a pair of blue jeans. He looked divine.

Why did I continue to find myself in embarrassing situations? I glanced at my dirt-encrusted overalls. "Uh, pruning?" *Sorry, Lord. Another untruth.* Remorse rose in my chest.

"What are you looking for?"

I never could get anything past him. I sighed. "Diamonds. I didn't find anything. I'm trying to figure out what my nighttime prowler is looking for."

"Maybe it isn't in the rosebushes."

"It isn't." I glanced around at the holes beneath what I'd hoped would be my blue ribbon winners. "I wasted an entire afternoon."

"Something learned is never wasted." Ethan took up the shovel I'd discarded. "If you'll get us something to drink, I'll fill these holes for you. Oh, and you have dirt across your face. It's kind of cute."

Dirt? Horror. I sprinted for the house and into the bathroom. Sure enough, a wide swath of dirt cut across my face. I pulled off my gardening gloves and tossed them in the corner. Then I grabbed a washcloth from the side of the tub and dabbed at the dirt, trying in vain not to wipe away my makeup. I couldn't face Ethan without my bravery mask. And I definitely couldn't change my clothes. He'd think I was trying to impress him.

I tossed the rag into the sink with disgust and took my dirt-covered, smeared face back to the kitchen. Upon opening the refrigerator, I discovered a pitcher of lemonade. I set the pitcher on the counter and grabbed two glasses from the cabinet next to the sink. My gaze fell upon Uncle Roy's toolshed.

That's it! The misplaced shovel. Leaving the drinks where they sat, I bolted out the back door, letting the screen slam behind me. Ethan called my name. The sound of a *thud* reached me as the shovel hit the ground.

Uncle Roy always left his toolshed unlocked so neighbors could borrow whatever they needed. Occasionally, a tool would stay at someone else's home, but Uncle Roy believed in sharing, no matter whether the user returned the item.

I threw the shed door open with a bang and peered into the dim recesses of the wooden building. Shovels, hoes, and rakes found a home in a plastic trash bin, while many implements I couldn't name hung from neat pegs on one of the walls. Uncle Roy's assorted plastic bins sat stacked in the corner. The perfect quick hiding place.

Ripping the lid from the top bin, I shoved my arm deep into birdseed. A fit of sneezing seized me, and Ethan gently moved me aside.

"Here. My arms are longer. What exactly am I expecting to find? If it's a mouse, I'll deal severely with you later." He plunged his hand into the seed until his elbow disappeared.

Ethan, afraid of mice? I covered my hand to stifle a

giggle. I found mice cute. Especially the small gray ones with big eyes and ears.

"Aha!" Ethan pulled out a navy coverall. "This it?"

Had to be. I stepped forward and took the clothing from his hand. "I'm pretty sure this is what my nocturnal predator wears." I held it against me, delighted to see it was several sizes too big. This didn't mean, necessarily, that the person wasn't female, just that he or she wore a larger size than I did.

"They must've changed here for easy access. Less obvious than if they're walking the streets in everyday clothes." Ethan turned and scanned the walls.

"If you dig deeper, you might find something else." I tossed the coverall on a shelf. "Maybe the other garden glove."

"No, I think we should call Joe."

"That could take an hour! If we find something, we'll put it back."

Ethan shook his head. "We've messed things up enough. You're inviting the wrath of Joe." He pulled his cell phone from his pocket and punched in a set of numbers.

I wasn't afraid of my cousin.

While Ethan occupied himself calling Joe, I shoved my arm into the bin with enough enthusiasm that seed spilled over the top. Within seconds, I came up clutching a blue-flowered gardening glove. I shoved it back inside, avoiding Ethan's glare.

I lay in bed that night with the investigation book lying open beside me and warm feelings for Ethan in my heart. He'd been angry with me for continuing my search. It didn't help that my hunch about the shed had proven true.

Ethan and Joe had both made a big deal about why God had burdened them with a knucklehead like me. I knew neither of them could stay mad forever. But I promised to think before acting in the future.

The next morning dawned bright. I woke with a stiff neck that couldn't keep me from following up on what I'd read in my *Dolt* book the night before. I'd scanned the table of contents and decided to start with neighborhood investigation. I had to work that day, so the street where the candy store sat would have to do as my neighborhood. The major goal for the day—the jewelry store and the newspaper.

One of the things I'd have to work on, according to the book, was getting my suspect to like me. This wouldn't be hard with Ruby and Mabel. They already did. Terri Lee, on the other hand, might be a challenge.

Aunt Eunice and I whipped up a batch of butterscotch fudge before I took off my apron. I would've liked for her to go with me to interrogate Ruby and Mabel, but after her outburst the other day, I changed my mind. I'd been honest about wanting to stop by the jewelry store and could tell by the inquisitive look on her face that she was dying to know why.

Before she had a chance to get nosy, I headed out the front door and down the sidewalk. Shadow Jewelers stood one block over in an impressive redbrick-fronted building. Opening the glass doors with brass trim, I heard soft music playing in the background. I stepped farther in and inhaled the pleasant aroma of something floral.

Terri Lee wasn't behind the counter. A rather plump woman masked in pancake makeup greeted me with a huge smile that didn't reach her eyes. "Welcome. How may I help you?"

"Is Terri Lee in?"

"Are you a friend of hers?" The woman looked down her nose at me and curled her lip. I smoothed my hand down my jeans, wishing I'd worn something classier.

"More like an acquaintance." How could I get this woman to let me see Terri Lee without arousing suspicion? "I'm interested in possibly having her design a piece of jewelry for me."

"How wonderful, but I'm afraid Terri Lee isn't in. Apparently she's picking up a shipment of supplies for her jewelry as we speak. Would you like to leave your number?"

"No, thank you. I'll try to catch her another time." *Great. Strike one.*

Back on the sidewalk, I turned left, walked half a block, and entered the nondescript plaster building that housed Mountain Shadows' only newspaper. Ruby sat behind the receptionist desk, a Hollywood magazine in hand. She didn't look much happier to see me than the woman at the jewelry store.

"If this is about the pictures for the paper, Summer,

it isn't my fault." Ruby smacked the magazine on the desk. "Mabel hasn't written the story yet. The diamonds and the dead boy are bigger news."

"That's okay, Ruby. I figured it was something like that." Actually, I'd forgotten all about the pictures with everything else that had been going on. Now I'd practice my new investigative skills. "How did the guy die?"

Ruby leaned forward and lowered her voice. "Homicide. Stabbed multiple times in the back."

That would explain the blood on the gardening gloves. "Wow. Wasn't he here to see Terri Lee Rupert?"

"That's what the Ruperts claim, but if you ask me, that girl doesn't seem too broken up about her beau being dead. She's been making moon eyes at Ethan Banning. Oh, add the jailbird to the list of her prey."

An ice-cold fist gripped my heart. "Really?"

"Yep. Seen 'em with my own eyes, and you know nothing gets past these baby blues. Not ten minutes ago, she and Ethan strolled into the diner across the street."

I spun around. Would it be too obvious if I went over there for lunch? I didn't care. Aunt Eunice could handle the store for another half hour. "Do they have any suspects in the boy's death?"

"Not a one." She retrieved the magazine from the desktop. "I'd best be getting back to work. I wouldn't want anyone saying I don't earn my pay."

I turned to stare out the window at the red awning of Lou's Diner. The large plate-glass window sent off a glare in the noon sun, and I couldn't see anyone sitting inside. With a deep breath, I exited the newspaper office, crossed the street, and pushed through the swinging doors of the diner before I lost my nerve.

Ethan's laugh was the first sound I heard. Then he called my name as he waved me over. "Come sit with us." He motioned to the chair beside Terri Lee. "We haven't ordered yet."

"I'm ordering takeout." Now why did I say that? Why did I insist on being antisocial with Terri Lee around? There was no reason I couldn't sit with them. I could've interrogated her. And watched Ethan's reaction.

"Are you sure? We've plenty of room." My gaze zeroed in on the fine laugh lines around his eyes, and it took everything I had to shift my attention to Terri Lee. "I stopped by the jewelry store today. Thought maybe the two of us could get better acquainted. The lady behind the counter said you were picking up a shipment of gems."

"That's true. High-quality diamonds. Several first-water quality." Terri Lee smoothed a napkin across her lap. "I plan on picking them up after lunch."

First-water quality? Sounds impressive. "Aren't you afraid of carrying diamonds around? Especially after someone buried a pile of them in my yard?"

"They did?" She pierced me with a gaze of steel.

"Oh, you hadn't heard? Must've happened before you came to town. Whoever buried the diamonds left a bundle of cash, too." I gave her a thin-lipped smile. "Hope to see more of you. Bye, Ethan." I left the diner before it occurred to me I hadn't purchased anything for lunch.

Within seconds, my cell phone rang. A glimpse of the caller ID showed Ethan. My heart skipped a beat. I was in trouble. "Hello."

"What were you trying to prove? Why must you be so rude?"

"Was I?" I leaned against the wall of a store a couple of doors down and stared at the sky. For someone exhibiting signs of jealousy, I wasn't gaining any points with the object of my affection. My throat tightened.

"You know you were. Terri Lee could use a friend. She just moved back to town."

"I said I went by the jewelry store to get to know her." I studied the cuticle of my thumb.

"You're acting very strange, Summer."

"Are you still sitting there with her? Please tell me you aren't speaking to me this way in front of someone." The thought hurt.

"Of course not. I excused myself and said I was going to the men's room." His sigh sounded heavy through the phone. "You all but accused her of knowing about the diamonds."

"Well, she's a likely suspect. She could profit from the diamonds. And don't forget, she's supposedly meeting someone to get a shipment. Most people wouldn't let it be known they were picking up a fortune in diamonds."

"You're impossible." He sighed again. "Did you apologize to Joe about messing up his crime scene?"

Oops. I'd forgotten. Kind of on purpose.

"Summer?"

"No, I didn't. I don't want him to keep me from searching. I want to see whether the person comes back."

"That's dangerous! We don't know what kind of person we're dealing with." The conversation ended.

I poked my head around the corner to make sure Ethan didn't follow me and headed toward the police station. If Ethan wanted to be a goody-goody, I had some groundwork to do. And fast.

I marched west to the newly constructed brick police station. In the reception area sat one of my neighbors, a widow by the name of Mrs. Hodge.

"Good morning, Mrs. Hodge."

"I wish I could say the same, Summer."

"Is everything all right?" I plopped into the vacant plastic seat next to her.

Mrs. Hodge twisted a white handkerchief in her thick, veined hands. "Twice within the last few nights, someone has trampled across my garden." She leaned toward me. "Once I could've sworn they stared in my bathroom window. I can't handle a Peeping Tom, Summer. I just can't." Tears welled in the old woman's eyes.

"I don't blame you." I patted her hand. The skin felt dry beneath my fingers. "I'm sure the police department can help you." *And maybe I can get some clues. So far, this neighborhood investigating is paying off.* "If you don't mind, I'd like to come by tonight and take a look around. Someone's been doing the same to me. Maybe we share a nighttime visitor."

"Oh, sweetie, I'd sleep so much better tonight if you checked things out for me. Bring your handsome boyfriend with you. You two looked lovely at the ball."

My boyfriend? I wish.

"Summer."

I glanced up into the stern face of my cousin Joe.

"Excuse me, Mrs. Hodge." I leaned to whisper in her ear. "I'll see you tonight. Around dark."

"Thank you." A tear slid down the old woman's cheek. "I'll make tea."

My heart ached at her apparent loneliness. I resolved

to make an effort to visit more often.

After patting her shoulder, I stood as tall as my petite frame would allow and planted fists on my hips. "Yes, Joe."

He cocked his head toward his office and spun on one heel, leading the way. Yep, I was in trouble.

Joe's office, actually a corner of the large room, was set apart with padded partitions. I sat straight backed in another plastic chair, crossed my ankles, and stared at the red-faced man in front of me. It seemed obvious he was losing the battle to control his temper. His face turned an unbecoming shade of cherry red.

"Settle down, Joe, before you have a heart attack."

After taking a deep breath, Joe fell into his chair. "Whatever you're doing—stop."

"I'm not doing anything, except asking a few questions. That's not against the law, is it?" I lifted a leg and crossed it over my knee. My foot jiggled a mile a minute.

"Ethan called me. You contaminated my crime scene. Your fingerprints are everywhere."

"I live there, Joe."

"Tampering with evidence is against the law. And you're getting mighty close to doing just that. If you find something, leave it alone."

The foot moved faster. "So arrest me." *Please, don't arrest me.* Having a criminal in the family would mortify Aunt Eunice and Uncle Roy. "Did you find anything else when you searched?"

"I'm not going to arrest you, and no, I didn't." He scrubbed a hand across his buzz cut. "Look. I'm not stupid enough to think you'll stay out of this. Just promise me that when you find things that pertain to this case, you'll tell me, okay? Without touching them. Also, I want you to be careful, and don't involve my girl."

His girl? My grin reached from one ear to the next. "You're calling April your girl? That's sweet." My feet fell to the floor. "If you're finished with me, I've got to get back to work. I'll let you know when I learn anything of importance."

"Don't forget what I told you."

I left the police station, turned right, and came face-to-face with Duane Parker, wearing of all things, navy coveralls. My mouth dried, and I swallowed against the cottony feeling. "Hello, Duane."

"Summer." His smile resembled a grimace. Eyes the color of Mississippi mud glared at me. Okay, the guy never got over my rejecting him as my date for the prom.

"How's it feel being back?" *Missing any coveralls?*

"Fine." Big talker, this one.

"Okay, bye." I waved good-bye and turned to run smack into a wall named Ethan. "Oh, it's you." I peered around him. "Where's your lunch date?"

"Terri Lee wasn't my lunch date." Ethan grasped my elbow and dragged me across the street to a bench beneath an oak tree. "If I didn't know any better, I'd think you were jealous."

"Of what?"

Ethan laid an arm across the back of the bench and handed me a paper sack. "You left the diner without ordering. I took the liberty of getting you a BLT."

"My favorite. Thanks." I grabbed the bag and peered inside, delighted to see a slice of carrot cake beside the sandwich.

"I know." Ethan turned toward me. "Summer, I'm sorry I went to Joe about you finding that glove in the birdseed, but I'm worried about you. I don't want anything to happen to you."

"Yeah, I know. I'm your Tinkerbell." *Why can't I be something more to him, Lord?*

"It's not just that." He took a deep breath and ran a hand through his curls, sending them into disarray. "Oh, never mind." He rose. "Enjoy your lunch. I'll talk to you later."

"Wait." I laid the sandwich on the bench. "Not just what?"

Ethan turned and waved. "It's nothing. Forget it."

A pigeon landed on the bench and pecked at my sandwich. "Stop it." I clapped my hands then turned as Ethan disappeared down the street. The bird swooped again, this time stealing a bite of the sandwich. I plopped back onto the bench. That wonderful man noticed I hadn't eaten. *Is it possible he cared more than I thought? But what about Terri Lee?*

A quick glance at my watch showed I'd been gone much longer than planned. I grabbed the brown sack with the cake and tossed it in a nearby garbage can. I'd lost my appetite.

Ethan's words stayed with me the rest of the day. I made candy while existing in a fog, mixing ingredients wrong. At one point, I spilled a pan of corn syrup down the front of the stove. Aunt Eunice lost her patience and tried to send me home. I declined and immersed myself in my work.

I knew I was a great candy maker. Fantastic, in fact. But this diamond case and being preoccupied with Ethan had my mind everywhere but where it needed to be. On my candy.

During the drive home, I mentally ran through my suspect list. Regardless of what Ethan thought, Terri Lee remained at the top. My number one. My unsub. The possible perp. But then again, Ruby knew an awful lot about the dead young man, and I had yet to interrogate Mabel. Then there was Duane.

I pounded a fist on the steering wheel. I'd completely forgotten to ask Ruby to show me her diamond ring. That could've led to a whole round of new questions. Maybe I wasn't cut out to be an investigator after all.

Besides, Ethan, Uncle Roy, Aunt Eunice, and Joe would all tell me to stick to candy making.

After I'd finished helping Aunt Eunice clean up after supper and changed into a clean summer dress, I grabbed my digital camera. If I'd been any kind of investigator before now, I already would've used it. I also grabbed a pencil and a pad of paper. With these investigative tools in hand, I strolled across the rural highway and hiked the quarter mile to our nearest neighbor, Mrs. Hodge.

I could have driven, I suppose, but I didn't want to miss a thing. My eyes scanned the ditch on each side of the tree-lined road as I zigzagged across the centerline. Nothing. Bits of garbage. A sickly sweet smell.

Searching the ditch, I found the source of the odor. A dead armadillo that made my stomach hitch. No footprints, diamonds, or cash. Not that I really expected to find anything, but I needed to keep my eyes open and my wits alert. I didn't need a "dummy" book to tell me that.

Mrs. Hodge's periwinkle blue–and–white wood-paneled cottage sat about fifty yards from the road, surrounded by a thick clump of trees. Shutters painted a darker shade of blue were shut tight against the summer evening sun. Thick foliage lined the road opposite her home.

My knock on the blue raised-panel door went unanswered for several minutes. As I turned to leave, curtains twitched at the window, and Mrs. Hodge's face peered out. I gave a cheerful wave.

"Summer, my dear!" Mrs. Hodge spoke before she had the door completely open. She snaked out a hand, grabbed my arm, and pulled me inside. She was amazingly strong for an elderly woman. "I have tea and cookies."

I pulled myself free and rubbed my arm where she'd squeezed. "Maybe I should look around outside first."

"If you think so." Mrs. Hodge led the way through a tiny kitchen and into a lush garden. Plants, bushes, and trees crowded the house and grew up and over trellises, arches, and a cobblestone sidewalk. A wooden fence surrounded the yard.

"I had no idea you had such a beautiful garden, Mrs. Hodge. This is a paradise." My eyes couldn't take it all in. I experienced strong feelings of envy over the roses growing there. Every color God and man could come up with, and the aroma welcomed me.

"It's what I do now that I'm alone. My plants are my friends. There's little enough for me to do since my son moved out and my husband died."

"I didn't know you had a son."

"We all have a past, don't we? Thank the good Lord He gives us the opportunity to become new. My son and I are estranged." The woman's shoulders heaved as she sighed. "I haven't seen him in years. Since before I moved to Mountain Shadows."

"Well, there's definitely plenty of room for someone to hide. It must be scary at night." I shuddered, thinking of the shadows that would appear once the sun went down.

"I could never be afraid of my plants." She grasped my arm again. "Over here. I found some footprints."

Beneath the kitchen window was a distinct set of prints imbedded in the soft soil of a flower bed.

I couldn't help but wonder why the diamond thief hadn't used Mrs. Hodge's garden instead of mine. The cache could've gone undiscovered for years in this jungle. And I wouldn't have lost what I'd hoped would be a prize-winning rose.

I snapped a picture of the footprints to give to Joe, since I'd neglected to photograph the prints outside my own house. It'd be interesting to see whether they matched. "How often have you felt someone watching you?"

"Three or four times a week. Now I keep my shutters closed. A shame really. I can't enjoy my friends this way. Are you ready for cookies now?"

I nodded and followed her inside. An unshuttered kitchen window with bright yellow-and-white-checkered curtains hung above the sink. I didn't need to search around the house to know this would be the only window the peeper looked through.

"My suggestion would be to get a lock for your gate." I took a seat at her yellow dinette. The vinyl crackled beneath me. "Have you noticed any other suspicious activity around here? Maybe in the woods across the street?"

Mrs. Hodge paused while pouring my tea. "Now that you mention it, yes. A few days ago, I'd been sitting on my front porch, sipping some chamomile tea. I swear I saw a flashlight beam in the woods across the road. I thought I heard loud voices, too. The wind was up that night, so I can't be sure."

She finished pouring and took a seat across from me. "There have been cars driving up and down the road at all hours. The headlights keep me awake. Why, do you think?"

I shrugged. "Someone's been snooping around my place." My stomach protested my lack of lunch. I grabbed a macaroon from the plate in the center of the table. "I'm wondering whether it could be the same person." I hadn't missed the fact she had mentioned voices. That meant more than one. "Could you tell whether the voices you heard were male or female?"

She shook her head. "I couldn't swear in court that I heard them at all. The wind was too strong."

I visited until dusk, eating cookies and drinking tea, but learned nothing new. My hostess seemed reluctant to let me go, and to ease her mind, I walked the perimeter of her property with a borrowed flashlight. Another beneficial investigative tool I'd need. And I added a sturdy aluminum briefcase to my list of things to buy. I'd need somewhere to store my tools.

True to my suspicions, the garden scared me. A soft

breeze rustled the branches overhead. In some places, the shadows were inky where the rising moonlight failed to penetrate the foliage. Once I reached the center of the garden, footsteps padded along the path.

I ducked behind some low-lying juniper bushes and flicked off my flashlight. I wouldn't classify this part of investigating as my favorite. My hands shook, and my legs trembled. I held my breath for fear of discovery.

Peter Langley, an elderly man I'd known since childhood, tiptoed past my hiding spot. He reminded me of Ichabod Crane. He glanced from side to side and slunk up to Mrs. Hodge's kitchen window.

I sprang and shone the flashlight at his face. "Mr. Langley."

"Summer? W—what are you d—doing here?" Mr. Langley's stutter grew worse as his nervousness elevated.

"I could ask you the same thing."

The back porch light came on, illuminating the garden. "Are you all right, Summer?" Mrs. Hodge stuck her head around the door frame.

"Just fine, Mrs. Hodge. I've found your Peeping Tom. Or Peter, rather." My chest swelled with my first investigative success.

Mr. Langley stuck his hands in his pockets and turned to face Mrs. Hodge. "I'm sorry, Mae."

"Peter, what are you doing sneaking around my garden at night?" Mrs. Hodge planted fists on her bony hips.

"I—I just wanted to see you. That's all."

"But why peek in the window? Why not knock on the door?"

He shrugged and scuffed his feet.

Seems I'd discovered a secret admirer rather than a criminal. Regardless, Peter Langley would be added to my list of suspects. No one who peered into women's windows could be considered blameless. I lowered my beam from his face.

"All you needed to do was call, Peter." The object of Mr. Langley's affection held the door wide. "Come on in."

Forgotten, I left the flashlight on the top step of the porch. The couple's voices drifted to me through the door. I smiled before rounding the house. Seemed everyone was finding love but me.

I hadn't gone far before I regretted leaving the flashlight. A country highway gets mighty dark at night, even with the moon and stars. Bullfrogs serenaded from a nearby pond, and the last of the evening's lightning bugs flickered off.

Halfway home, I spotted the welcome beams of an approaching vehicle and stepped to the side of the road. The car swerved toward me, and I dove into the ditch. I lifted my head. A dark-colored, four-door sedan disappeared over the hill before I could catch a glimpse of the license plate.

8

Rocks and thorns bit into my knees and palms. I planted my hands under me and pushed to my feet. I groaned and collapsed in a puddle beside the road, literally. Standing water from our last rain soaked through my skirt. My ankle throbbed. Great. What a mess I'd gotten myself into this time.

Another set of headlights cut through the night, this time coming from the opposite direction. My pulse beat heavy in my throat, threatening to choke me. The truck passed then backed up and stopped within a few feet of where I sat.

Horror. No, not Ethan! I was in trouble. Again.

"Summer!" The slam of his truck door reverberated through the darkness. "What happened? Are you all right?"

"I fell in the ditch and twisted my ankle."

Without another word, I found myself swept into the arms of the man I loved and deposited in his truck as gently as a piece of fine china. Perfect if my face didn't burn from humiliation.

Once more in the driver's seat, Ethan's knuckles turned white from his grip on the steering wheel. He took a deep breath, asked God to guide his words, and turned to me. "What are you doing walking the highway in the dark?" He spoke each word, separate and distinct. His hands remained on the wheel, obviously in a valiant attempt to keep from strangling me.

"Mrs. Hodge asked me to visit."

"At this time of night?"

"We had tea and cookies. It took awhile." Soon he'd painfully extract all the information from me. Like a dentist pulling teeth.

"I saw her at the police station earlier today. She thought someone was watching her. I thought it might be the same person who's been hanging around my house." My knees burned. Probably scraped, as they often were when I was a child.

Ethan glanced up. "Why me, God?"

I frowned. "She invited me over for tea, cookies, and a look around. My first successful investigation. It wasn't a stalker. Seems old Mr. Langley has a crush on Mrs. Hodge. It's cute, don't you think?"

He pierced me with his stare then put the truck in drive.

"I dropped my camera and notepad in the ditch. Can you get them for me before we go?"

He exhaled sharply from his nose and jammed the truck back into park. While he searched for my equipment, I studied my knees in the light of the dashboard. Yep, I'd scraped them. Badly. Blood trickled around several small pebbles stuck in my skin. I raised one leg to examine my ankle, which was swelling. I'd be limping tomorrow. Hopefully, Uncle Roy still had his cane from when he'd had foot surgery.

Ethan returned and tossed my retrieved items on the seat between us. "What aren't you telling me, Summer? There's always something you leave out."

The man knows me so well. And, since I'd kind of made a promise to God not to lie anymore, I spilled my guts. "A car swerved toward me. A big car. I think they tried to run me over. On purpose. I had to jump out of the way and fell in the ditch." *Please, have mercy on me.*

A muscle twitched in Ethan's clenched jaw. He spun gravel as the truck roared back onto the highway. "You're not going to leave this alone, are you?"

"I can't, Ethan. Not now. I'm involved."

He drove me home in silence. Once we arrived, Ethan swept me into his arms. I couldn't help but wish it were under different circumstances. He carried me into the house, calling for Aunt Eunice. Truly whimpered and jumped against Ethan's legs.

She took one look at me, dirty and disheveled, and shrieked. "What happened? Oh, Lord, help us!"

Ethan deposited me on the counter beside the sink and sat in the nearest chair, leaving me to Aunt Eunice's ministrations. He propped his elbow on the table and rested his handsome head in his hand.

I had to admit to a certain sense of embarrassment at having him leave me on the counter like a five-year-old, but I wasn't in any condition to argue with a man who resembled a marble statue. Without lifting his head, he raised his eyes to peer at me before closing them. The pain there hurt more than the scrapes on my knees or the throbbing of my ankle.

He turned away from me. "I'm calling Joe."

Aunt Eunice scrubbed my knees clean, wrapped my ankle with an Ace bandage, and started a pot of tea. Her cure for everything. I slid from the counter, reaching my good foot to the floor. I hobbled to the front porch, deciding the matter between me and Ethan warranted attention before changing from my muddy clothes. Ethan hung up the phone and followed me before taking my smarting hand in his large one and leading me outside.

Once I sat safely on the porch swing with pillows fluffed and propped behind my back, he took the seat beside me. He laid his arm along the back of the swing, and I curled into him, resting my head on his chest. I could've stayed there for the rest of my life, listening to his heartbeat and the rhythm of his breathing.

"Ethan, why won't you talk to me?"

"I don't know what to say." I strained to hear his words. "You scared me. When I saw you sitting on the side of the road. . ."

"I'm sorry. I'm fine."

His arm lowered to wrap around me. He pulled me tight to his side. I breathed in the manly scent of his cologne. I could've died happy right at that moment.

Uncle Roy roared up the drive and honked a greeting.

"Woman, you do beat all." Ethan squeezed then released me and stood. "You'll be the death of me." Ethan bent and planted a kiss on my forehead. "Your uncle's home. I'll leave you in his protection. Be careful. Please." With those words, he bounded from the porch and to his truck.

Darkness swallowed his taillights. I set the swing in motion with my good foot. Ethan had been frightened. His look in the kitchen seemed to be of a man who cared about a woman. My heart did cartwheels. *He cares for me. Dare I think it? Maybe even loves me?* Why wouldn't he open his mouth and say it outright?

"Where's Ethan?" Aunt Eunice pushed open the screen door, her hands busy with a tray of iced tea and cookies.

"He left." I accepted the tea and shook my head at the cookies. Baked goods had a habit of going straight to my hips, and I'd already had five cookies at Mrs. Hodge's. Aunt Eunice set the tray on the wooden patio table.

"I'm onto something, Aunt Eunice. I really think I am. Someone deliberately tried to run me over tonight. I'm sure of it."

Her hand flew to cover her heart. "Did you see who it was?"

"No. It was too dark to get a good look at the car." I sipped my tea. "What I'm wondering, though, is why the diamonds were stashed in our yard rather than Mrs. Hodge's. She's got a jungle in her backyard."

"That garden is her world." Aunt Eunice brushed cookie crumbs from her bosom. "Our yard is easily accessible. The river runs behind Mae's yard; then there's her fence. We've got a cleared yard and woods in the back to hide in."

"Mrs. Hodge did mention she thought she heard voices arguing a few nights back."

"Really? Way out here?" Eunice lowered herself into a rocking chair. "I'm thinking the woods behind our house might warrant some exploring. I'll get your Uncle Roy to help. He needs something else to do besides spending so much time at that nursery of his."

"Tonight?" Fatigue weighed me down. The thought of traipsing through the dark woods on a bum ankle wasn't my idea of fun.

Aunt Eunice glanced at my iodine-stained knees and bandaged ankle. "I guess not. You're in no condition. We couldn't see anything in the dark anyway."

I lifted my tea to my lips, as did my aunt. We

continued to swing, our feet pushing in unison. The squeaking mingled with the serenading of frogs and locusts, and I grew drowsy.

———

My aches and pains caught up with me the next morning. Debating whether to stay in bed, I chose to get up, despite a stiff back and aching joints. I felt ninety rather than nearing thirty. Dear Aunt Eunice had propped Uncle Roy's cane within easy reach, and I used it to hobble into the bathroom.

Getting into the shower required an art of body manipulation. I was almost tempted to call Aunt Eunice to help me. Memories of her cleaning my wounds last night as if I were a child dissuaded me. I didn't need her scrubbing my back.

I decided on a bath, hoping the hot water would melt away the pain. As I settled back into the warm cocoon of a tub full of bubbles, I prayed. Maybe late in the game, but I figured better late than never when asking for God's help.

I prayed for wisdom, discernment, and protection until the water grew too cool for comfort. I emerged with a sense of renewed purpose, peace, and slightly less stiff muscles. The appetizing aroma of sizzling bacon drifted up the stairs, causing me to don my clothes as quickly as standing on one foot would allow.

Making my way down the stairs required balance and nerves of steel. Especially with an excited dog frolicking around my legs. A fine sheen of perspiration dotted my upper lip by the time I reached the kitchen.

Aunt Eunice greeted me with a chipper grin. "Good morning, Hopalong." I winced at her new endearment for me.

"Good morning. Breakfast smells good." I sank into the nearest chair with a sigh.

"How are you feeling, sweetie?" Aunt Eunice placed my breakfast plate in front of me. Did she have me confused with my uncle? I'd never be able to eat an entire omelet, toast, and bacon.

"Better. I don't think I'm up to any heavy cooking at the candy store today. I'll take up position behind the counter and let you do the hard stuff."

"Don't forget you need to dip the rest of those creams. You can do that sitting down." She fiddled with the kitchen faucet. "Your uncle still hasn't fixed this. I'll have to ask Ethan or Joe."

"You're right. I'll dip, and I'm sure they won't mind fixing the sink." Dipping would be easier than jumping up and down to wait on customers.

We bounced to work in Aunt Eunice's truck, the cane beside me. By the time we arrived, I couldn't have told which hurt my body more—landing in the ditch or riding in the truck.

The morning passed with as much speed as a snail. I dipped tray after tray of creams, putting the fancy letters on top, stifling yawns, and fighting drooping eyelids. I perked when the bell over the door tinkled.

In strolled Terri Lee, looking amazing in tight designer jeans and a vintage T-shirt. She'd swept her raven hair in a loose chignon. I strained to see what shoes she wore. They were the most adorable pair of royal blue ballet slippers. I shoved aside my shoe envy and grabbed my cane. Only Terri Lee could make jeans and a T-shirt look glamorous.

Her glossy pink lips curled into a sneer. "Did you hurt yourself? I'm so sorry."

"Just a little sprain. I'll be fine." I glanced out the window, trying to get a glimpse of her car. I had a strong suspicion she was the one who'd tried to run me over. I couldn't spot anything other than Aunt Eunice's clunker.

I motioned to my aunt that I'd wait on Terri Lee and limped to the counter. "What can I get for you?"

"A three-pound box of dark chocolate creams." The woman actually giggled. "They're Ethan's favorites, I've heard."

God had to rein me in. I wanted to hurl the box and bounce it off her head. "Yes, they are. Would you like the box wrapped?"

"Of course." She gave me a thin smile and handed me her credit card. "Ethan and I are going to dinner at that new seafood restaurant. Since he's paying, I'd like to get him dessert."

I bet you would.

They're going out on a date? Did the woman collect men like shoes? My heart plummeted, landing with a thud. I wrapped her gift in the most attractive paper we carried—a pristine white with subtle stripes—and tied it with a silver ribbon. The candy was still for the man I loved. I wanted it to look nice. After all, he'd know it came from my store.

I thanked her for her purchase. She glided out the door with a merry wave. I turned and locked myself in the bathroom for the next fifteen minutes, battling tears.

Had I imagined Ethan's feelings last night? Was I seeing only what I wanted to see? But I'd been so sure.

Placing my hands palms down on the restroom vanity, I stared at my reflection in the mirror. *Why, Lord? Why couldn't Ethan return my feelings? If he's not the man for me, why can't I find someone else? Why won't You take away this desire?*

With a heavy heart, I hobbled back to the dipping machine. Aunt Eunice waited on customers. Despite my melancholy mood, I thanked God for the continuing support for Summer Confections. During one customer's visit, my ears perked up at the mention of a newcomer to town.

"He's new at Mountain Shadows Fellowship," the woman went on to explain. "He's looking for a job. Something besides coffee barista. Good-looking young man. Pleasant with the thickest brown hair I've seen in a long time."

Well, I'd identified my mystery man from church. I wondered if he had anything to do with the recent crime spree. He'd make as good a suspect as anyone. I sighed and turned off the dipping machine. I was getting nowhere fast on this case. Other than having an unidentified vehicle almost run me over, absolutely nothing was happening. I wasn't even sure if my near miss had anything to do with the diamonds.

Then, speaking of the devil, in strolled the man. The previous customer had been on the right track. He had dark chocolate eyes and thick, wavy hair the color of the rich mud of the South. My breath hitched when I got a close-up look at the man.

He sauntered up to Aunt Eunice and held out a hand.

"I'm Nate Landon, and it's a pleasure to meet you."

"I'm Eunice, and back there is my niece, Summer." Aunt Eunice simpered like a schoolgirl. "What can I do for you?"

"I'm making the rounds, introducing myself. Heard this place made the best fudge in the world. Thought I'd try it for myself. I'll take a pound." Nate leaned against the counter, his eyes remaining fixed on me. I couldn't help but put up a hand to smooth any stray hair. *Horror!* Chocolate covered my fingers. Not my usual type of hair gel.

Aunt Eunice thrust the fudge into his hands. "First order's on the house."

Nate snickered. "Ladies, it's my privilege." The man actually bowed before exiting the store.

Aunt Eunice swooned. Her hand fluttered to her forehead as she draped herself over the counter. "If only I were thirty years younger. Hubba hubba!"

"You're married." I rose from the dipping stool to wash my hands.

"I can still see, girlie." Her eyes widened. "You've got chocolate in your hair."

"I know." I tried stomping to the bathroom, winced at the pain in my ankle, and resorted to sulking as I pushed open the door. The sink seemed suddenly tiny. No way would my head fit under the faucet.

I grabbed a handful of paper towels and shoved them under running water then started the laborious job of pulling chocolate out of my curly hair. Great. One side now lay flat against my head, while the other curled in a riotous auburn display. *Please, Lord, don't let Mr. GQ visit the store again today.*

9

I sat in the coffee bar the following Sunday nursing my favorite mocha and staring with hungry eyes at Ethan as he laughed at something Terri Lee said. *Yep, it's time to move on.* The thought stabbed me in the heart. I pursed my lips around the straw, sipped—and slurped as Nate slid into the seat beside me.

He had made a habit of visiting the candy store each day since his first stop. Sometimes to make a purchase, more often to talk. He focused his conversations on Aunt Eunice but centered his attention on me. To be honest, the attention flattered me. I'd mooned after Ethan for so long that I'd put dating on a back burner.

"Good morning, Summer."

"Good morning, Nate." I took a daintier sip of my coffee and tried not to notice Ethan watching us.

"Summer." Nate placed a hand over mine. His were soft, not the working hands Ethan possessed. "I'm hoping you'd do me the honor of having dinner with me tonight."

"Dinner?" I yanked my gaze from Ethan and stared into the dark depths of Nate's eyes.

"I know we don't know each other well, but maybe we could remedy that with a quick meal at the diner to get to know each other better."

"Uh, I, uh—" Terri Lee's giggle drifted to me. I could not think of a single reason not to go out with Nate.

His face split with a broad grin, and he rose from his chair. "Great. I'll pick you up at five."

My eyes threatened to burst with tears. I mourned something I'd never had. I raised my gaze. Ethan stared at me, frowning. I lowered my head and rushed into the sanctuary seeking solace in the arms of my heavenly Father.

Since the diner ranked a three on the casual scale, I dressed in a pair of linen drawstring pants and tailored blouse for dinner. Aunt Eunice giggled like a teenager when I told her who'd invited me. Although I knew the scenery across the table would be nice, I couldn't drum up a drop of excitement.

The doorbell rang, and Truly flew to the front door, vibrating the walls with her shrill barks. Aunt Eunice opened the door and ushered Nate inside. I took a deep breath and went to join them.

Nate stood at the foot of the stairs, one hand resting on the banister. He held a fistful of carnations in his other hand. I had to admit, the guy acted like a gentleman and he oozed charm. As I reached the bottom of the stairs, the bell rang again, sending Truly into a frenzy.

Ethan stood peering through the glass panel. He didn't look happy.

Aunt Eunice bustled from the kitchen, glancing at Nate before she opened the front door and stepped aside. "Ethan! How nice to see you."

"Eunice." He nodded at her. "Nate. Summer." He extended a hand to Nate. "Y'all going somewhere?"

"To the diner." Nate accepted the offered hand, clearly not perceptive to the tension in the air. "Summer accepted my invitation to dinner."

Ethan's eyes turned to blue ice. "Great. Have a good time." He turned to Aunt Eunice. "Roy said you were having problems with a leaky faucet?"

"Yes. In the kitchen."

I forced a smile, and Nate ushered me from the house. That's the kind of luck I had. The kind where Ethan would show up as I left on a date. I mentally kicked myself. Why should I care if he was upset? Didn't he just go out with Terri Lee?

Nate kept up a running conversation during the short drive into town. I tried to pay attention. Really. But if there was to be a test on what he talked about while he drove, I'd flunk it.

Cars jammed the parking lot outside the diner when we pulled up. Some of them with drivers casting curious glances our way and shouting greetings. And still Nate talked. I'd never met a man who spewed words the way he did. And all along he remained a gentleman, steering me with a hand on my elbow in the direction he wanted me to go.

The hostess seated us in a booth in the far corner. After stepping aside for me to slide in, Nate scooted in next to me. Okay, now I was uncomfortable. It'd been so long since I'd been on a date I wasn't sure how to react. So, I said nothing. I'd been mooning over Ethan so long that I hadn't been interested in anyone else.

"Would you like me to order for you?"

"No." I snapped my menu open. "I've been here plenty of times. I think I can order for myself."

"Wonderful." Despite my snappish attitude, his smile didn't fade.

The waitress arrived with glasses of ice water, and

Nate ordered meat loaf with the works. I asked for a chef salad. Before I knew it, Nate had placed his arm along the back of the booth. I stiffened and glared at the offending appendage.

"Does this bother you?"

"Yes, actually." I shifted in my seat to look at him. His being in such close proximity caused me to break into a sweat. "No offense, Nate, but I don't know you very well, and you're coming on kind of strong."

"You're right." He slid from the booth. "That's always been a problem of mine. Getting in people's personal space. I apologize. I meant no disrespect."

He did look embarrassed, and I felt twinges of guilt at being so rude. "No, I'm sorry." I offered up a sheepish smile.

Nate settled back against the seat opposite me. "So, how do you like working for your aunt?"

"Actually, she works for me. You wouldn't know it by the way she bosses me around, but that's the way we've always been. I love owning my own business. It's always been a dream of mine. Owning my own candy store."

I straightened to make room for the waitress to place my salad. "People are in a good mood when they come in to buy candy. I'd like to expand to a bakery someday. But that'll take a partner. I don't bake."

Nate slapped a hand on the table and laughed, rattling glasses. "You're a riot, Summer. I'm looking forward to getting to know you better."

Great. I shoved a forkful of salad in my mouth. I mean, he was gorgeous, but Nate seemed—fake. Too perfect. Too much of a gentleman. How many men go around wanting to hear all about the woman they're with?

I haven't met any, in fact. If I wasn't talking, he was. And the only time the man stopped talking was when he had food in his mouth. It made him suspicious in my mind. Untrustworthy and another name on my suspect list.

Then, to make my evening more complete, Terri Lee waltzed in. She caught a glimpse of us and made a beeline for our table. "Summer, who's your friend?" She cocked one hip and actually tossed her hair over her shoulder. I thought they only did that in movies. "I'm Terri Lee Rupert."

Call me crazy, but she looked at Nate as if they already knew each other. She seemed delighted to see him, and he seemed annoyed. Not at all like the man who'd asked me on this date.

"Terri Lee, this is Nate Landon. He's new to town."

"How nice." She blinded us with a thousand-watt smile, her white teeth flashing between ruby-red lips, and spun around to leave as quickly as she'd arrived.

Being the investigator I was quickly becoming, I studied Nate's face from behind my water glass. He'd stopped talking. Clue number one. Clue number two: the stormy look on his face. Yep. Terri Lee and Nate already knew each other, and things didn't look rosy in that corner. Was Nate also familiar with Mountain Shadows' ex-con, Duane? I shrugged. Why couldn't I just enjoy the attentions of a handsome man without thinking he had ulterior motives? He was a man; therefore he most likely knew Terri Lee. The woman had always gotten around. Even during high school.

After an obvious struggle to remain composed and restore the pleasant look on his face, Nate leaned across the table, took my hand in his, and said, "I heard things have been exciting at your place lately. Someone mentioned you'd found a fortune in diamonds."

I choked, spewing water across the table. "What?"

Nate removed his hand from mine and reached for a napkin. "It's all over town you'd found some diamonds on your property." He swiped the napkin across his face, removing the drops of water I'd sprayed.

"Actually, Ethan and I did." With great precision, I placed my glass on the table. "Why?"

"Just making small talk. How many were there?" Nate winked. "Did you keep some for yourself?"

My back stiffened. "No, I didn't." Although, God forgive me, I wanted to. "I turned them over to the police."

"Pity." Nate shrugged. "I would've liked to have seen them. I heard they're worth millions. With the right clarity—" He opened the dessert menu. "Dessert?"

I flipped through the menu, wondering why Nate invited me to dinner. "Did you invite me to dinner to grill me?"

"No." He looked taken aback. Hurt even. His eyes widened. "I wanted to get to know you. I noticed you at church. Asked about you. I'm just curious. It isn't every day someone finds that kind of loot. Enough to change someone's life. Those diamonds could buy you the bakery to add to your business."

"But they aren't mine." I couldn't help but remember how I'd thought the same thing.

"What if they're never claimed?"

Now that I hadn't thought of. Was there such a possibility? I chewed the inside of my lip. Nate was right. The money could completely rearrange my life. I'd have to check with Joe to see what would happen if no one made a claim.

Nate reverted to his charming, talkative self, and to my surprise, I agreed when he mentioned taking a walk downtown. The temperature hovered around ninety degrees. Folks smiled, waved, and called out greetings. I didn't pull away when Nate took my hand in his. He wasn't Ethan, but maybe if Ethan were lost to me, he'd be the next best thing.

The next few days, Nate showed up at the candy store around lunchtime and took me across the street to the diner. My heart still hitched whenever I spotted Ethan, but the dull throb slowly diminished. Funny thing is, despite Terri Lee's constant tales of their dating, I rarely saw them together.

When I did see Ethan, he seemed to watch Nate and me with eagle eyes. His gaze stayed glued on us as if he were a chaperone from the Victorian era. Nate didn't notice, or didn't care, but Ethan's scrutiny unnerved me.

The following Saturday happened to be the day for the annual Fourth of July picnic at the church. Months ago I'd volunteered to man the buffet tables with Ethan as my partner. Nate had agreed to organize a coed softball game.

The day burned as only a summer day in the Ozark Mountain foothills could, with the humidity hovering somewhere around 1,000 percent. I thanked God for the foresight to skip high fashion and wear shorts and a T-shirt. My flip-flops with the red, white, and blue tassels were as festive as I got.

Ethan appeared at my side with a battery-operated

fan. "I know it'll only blow around the hot air, but maybe we can fool ourselves into thinking it's cooler."

"Thank you. You're a godsend. Set it right there." I pointed to a spot in the center of the table. "That way we can oscillate it to hit both of us."

"Good idea." Our conversation screeched to a halt for the next hour. By then folks had arrived, laden with their offerings of food, and we were too busy serving to manage much more than an "Excuse me" or "Sorry" when we bumped into each other. How I wished he'd planned the bumps as a ploy to touch me.

Terri Lee arrived about halfway through the day, attired in what I could only describe as *almost dressed*. The shorts would've fit a five-year-old, and the halter top, well, let's say the red scrap of fabric covered only what it had to. And who wore heels to a picnic? If the woman wanted attention, her wish came true. Forks suspended in midair as men paused in shoveling their food to ogle her.

I sneaked a glance from the corner of my eye at Ethan and smiled. One quick look at Terri Lee, and he'd gone back to work. I was glad to know Ethan still guarded what went through his eyes and ears. Nate, on the other hand, stood on the pitcher's mound with his mouth hanging open. I wanted to stuff a ball in his gaping hole.

Ruby approached the table holding a plate out for a helping of potato salad, and my own mouth dropped to the ground. The diamonds sprinkled across the gold band she wore on her right hand had to add up to about three carats. My gaze traveled upward. She wore a necklace to match!

"Nice jewelry, Ruby."

"Thank you, Summer." She turned her hand to catch

the sun's light. "I know they're a bit much for a picnic, but you know a girl and her diamonds."

"Not really. Haven't had the pleasure." I plopped a healthy serving of salad on her plate. "Are they new?"

"Fairly new." She smiled her thanks and moved on to Ethan for a helping of fried chicken.

Once the line of people passed, I filled a plate of my own and sat in the nearest chair to enjoy my lunch. Ethan pulled up a seat of his own and joined me. We ate while listening to the good-natured jests coming from the ball field.

April giggled as she struck out, and Joe stepped up to wrap his arms around her on the pretense of showing her how to bat. I felt a certain amount of pride at having a part in getting them together.

My spine tingled, and I turned to face Ethan, finding him staring at me. His cobalt eyes looked sad. My heart lurched.

"Summer, I—"

Mabel's approach cut him off. She wore her camera slung around her neck. "I'm taking photos of the picnic. Smile, you two."

I gave her a closed-lipped smile and wished she'd go away.

"I'll be sure to get a copy to you." Mabel replaced her lens cap. "You look so good together."

Must she rub salt in my open wound? To make matters worse, Terri Lee sauntered over and leaned against the table.

"Hey, Ethan. Summer. I have to admit I've missed the simple fun of these picnics. Takes you back to it all, doesn't it?"

"Back to what?" I tossed my plate in the garbage.

"The simple life. Back to what really matters." She pushed forward and stood behind Ethan, her well-manicured hands massaging his shoulders. "Simple food, friends, and hope for the future."

Ethan stood, sliding free from her grasp. "Think I'll join that softball game. See the two of you later."

"That man." Terri Lee folded her arms across her chest. "He's an angel, isn't he?"

"Yes, he is." I stacked the dishes.

"He's the primary reason I'm sticking around this one-horse town."

"Uh-huh." *Him and about a dozen others.*

"How are you and Nate getting along? He's a looker."

"We're just friends." I took the pile of used paper plates and deposited them in the garbage. Then I turned, crossing my arms. "What do you want, Terri Lee?"

"What do you mean?"

"We aren't exactly bosom buddies. Why all the small talk?"

She leaned closer, whispering in my ear. "Just getting reacquainted with an old friend." Terri Lee removed the sunglasses she wore on top of her head and placed them over her eyes. "Enjoy the rest of the Fourth."

If her behind shook any harder as she sashayed away, the woman would've broken something. I couldn't help but wish she had. I spent the rest of the evening wondering what Ethan wanted to tell me.

Night fell around nine o'clock, and I spread a blanket on the ground to watch the fireworks. I sat cross-legged and looked around.

Families nearby also prepared for the night festivities. Mothers laid toddlers down to sleep, the soft grass a pillow beneath their heads. Older children squeezed in one last game of hide-and-seek, and Nate stretched out on the blanket beside me.

"The band will start up after the fireworks. Do you want to stay? I've heard they're pretty good." Nate tilted a bottle of water and drained it without stopping for air.

He wiped his forearm across his mouth. "It's hot."

I unfolded my legs and bent them in front of me, crossed my arms, and rested my chin on them. "Sure. Why not?"

"Something wrong, Summer?"

I forced a smile to my face. "No. I'm just resting."

"We don't have to stay. Not if you're too tired. I know you were on your feet all day."

I wished he'd shut up. How could I tell this man beside me that my heart still yearned for someone else? Nate grabbed another water bottle from the nearby cooler and handed it to me.

"Thank you."

"You're welcome." The fireworks exploded over our heads with a glorious array of color as Nate leaned in to kiss me. Over his shoulder, I noticed Ethan watching us. Somehow feeling as if I were betraying him, I closed my eyes.

10

I jerked back, my face flaming as shrieks rose above the boom of the fireworks. Ruby and Mabel stood nose to nose trying to shout over the other.

"They're mine!" Ruby's thin frame shook.

"Well, I found them! That makes them mine." Mabel folded her arms across her nonexistent bosom.

"You ain't nothing but a thief, Mabel. Admit it." Ruby stomped her foot.

"I'm not admitting any such thing, you old bird."

"Why you—"

Joe rose from the faded quilt he shared with April and approached the two women. He spoke in quiet tones until they stepped apart and went their separate ways, glaring over their shoulders at each other.

I couldn't help but wonder what they'd found that belonged to one and was claimed by the other. Nate's stare alternated between the two elderly women as they stalked to opposite sides of the darkened field. He continued watching until they passed from sight.

He must have felt my gaze on him, because he turned and smiled. "Interesting pair."

We remained silent as the fireworks built to their finale. Beneath the rainbow-colored fire in the sky, I pondered how I felt about Nate's kiss.

Pleasant, but not quite the wave-crashing kiss I expected from a man I was attracted to. There wasn't any passion. I licked my lips, tasting Nate's soda, and shrugged.

Fireworks over, I gathered up the threadbare blanket and tucked it under my arm. I no longer had any desire to stay. Standing, I surveyed the drowsy business of families preparing to leave. Babies slept on dads' shoulders. Toddlers whined, clutching at the shirts of mothers. My heart lurched as I spotted Joe bending to plant a tender kiss on April's lips. Her eyes closed, and she leaned into him. I sighed.

"You okay?" Nate took the blanket from my arm.

"Yes. Just tired." *And confused, sad, lonely—take your pick.*

"Let's get you home." He placed an arm around my shoulders and steered me toward the parked cars. I glanced behind us. Ethan stood watching. I tossed a wave and smiled, my heart lightened as he returned it before walking away. He thrust his hands into his pockets and, with hunched shoulders, disappeared into the shadows.

Nate and I caught up with Aunt Eunice and Uncle Roy. "I'll ride home with them, Nate. No reason for you to make the trip out of town."

"I don't mind, Summer." I couldn't read his face in the dark, but his voice sounded hurt, rejected.

"I know." I planted a quick kiss on his cheek. "I had a wonderful time." I retook the blanket and squeezed into the front of Uncle Roy's truck between him and my aunt. Through the rearview mirror, as we pulled away, I could make out Nate's form standing in the parking lot.

Aunt Eunice placed a hand on my knee. "Why didn't you let Nate bring you home, honey?"

I put my hand over hers. *Why indeed?* "Do you know of anything belonging to Ruby that Mabel may have claimed?"

A raised eyebrow told me she'd caught my ruse at changing the subject. "Can't say as I do. Roy, what about you?"

"Nope. But those two old hens always got something to bicker about. They're the best of friends, you know." He slowed and honked the truck's horn in greeting as we passed Duane on his nightly walk. The man whistled a tune I didn't recognize; then the sound was gone. Lost in the wind as we passed by.

"How can you say that?" I studied my uncle's profile. "All they do is fight."

"And they love every minute of it." Uncle Roy steered the truck into the drive. He turned to face me. "Mabel and Ruby have been friends since they were in school together. One wouldn't know what to do without the other. They need the bickering as much as they need the air they breathe."

"Hmm."

"Sweetie?" Aunt Eunice squeezed my leg. "What's up with you and that Nate fellow? You like the boy?"

I smiled at my aunt calling Nate a boy. "I haven't decided yet. I've liked Ethan for so long I'm not sure I'm ready for someone to step in and take his place in my heart. But I'm tired of waiting around for Ethan to make a move."

"God has someone for each of us. Don't rush ahead without asking Him what His plan for your life is." Aunt Eunice patted my knee. There she went again, telling me to wait for God's plan. Why did I find that so difficult to do?

Uncle Roy frowned and leaned forward, peering through the front window of the truck. "What in God's green earth?" He shoved the driver's side door open and bolted outside. "Summer, you might want to see this."

Rather than wait for Aunt Eunice to climb from the truck, I slid out Uncle Roy's door. The truck headlights bathed my rose garden. Or what was left of it anyway.

Someone had dug up every bush and tossed it aside like yesterday's leftovers. Tears wasted no time in welling and running down my cheeks. I dropped the blanket and ran to my slaughtered babies.

The garden resembled a forgotten graveyard. A cemetery for discarded dreams. I'd never have a rose worthy of competition now. Who would do such a thing? I turned to my aunt and uncle. "Why?"

"I don't know," Aunt Eunice replied. They stepped beside me, placing their arms around me.

"I do. Someone is looking for something. Whoever left the diamonds left something else. We haven't found what that is yet." My voice trembled with my anger.

I knelt beside my battered Midnight Blue rosebush and grasped the stalk. Placing the bush back in the hole, I scooped and patted the soil around its base then moved on to the next one. Without a word, my aunt and uncle knelt and performed the same administrations with the other rosebushes. "Wait. We need to let Joe see this."

Only time would tell whether the bushes would take root and survive the evening's brutal attack. I rose and, placing hands on my hips, popped the kinks from my back. My babies were back in their beds, for what it was worth. My knees were stiff from the caked mud, and I was glad for the darkness to cover the stains.

Wanting to ask God why this happened came to me first. But I knew. Someone was afraid I was getting too close. If only I knew as much as this person thought I did. Maybe the time had come to read some more in the *Dolt* book. I sighed and entered the house behind my aunt and uncle.

The stairs loomed in front of me. With heavy steps, I dragged myself up them and into my room. I shrieked.

Pillows without their stuffing lay strewed. White batting gave the effect of lumpy snow. Someone had slashed the mattress and pulled out wads of stuffing. Scattered books covered the floor. Drawers hung open with bits of my underwear hanging from them. I clenched my fists at my sides.

Uncle Roy thundered up the stairs, trusty rifle in his hands. He stopped and gaped at the mess. "Whoa. Girl, you got somebody running scared."

"You think?" Biting off the words, I set a hand on his shoulder before stepping inside the carnage. "I'm sorry. I shouldn't have said that." A sob caught in my throat. I wanted to break down and cry. I squared my shoulders, calling on God to give me strength. "Did you call Joe?"

Uncle Roy nodded. "Outside. He'll be here in about fifteen minutes."

I sighed.

"While I'm at it, I'll suggest he pack his bags and move in. He's been here enough lately." Uncle Roy took one more look around and left.

I took one step farther and whipped my gaze from one side to the other. "Where's Truly?" This time the sob escaped me, and I fell to my knees. Crawling through the debris in my room, I continued to cry her name.

No answer.

I jumped to my feet and bolted from the room,

down the stairs, and out the front door. "Truly!"

Swiping a hand across my streaming eyes, I cleared my vision and stumbled down the porch steps, banging my shin on a flowerpot. Pain radiated up my leg, and I clutched the hurt spot. That would definitely leave a mark. "Truly!"

Aunt Eunice joined me on the front lawn.

"I can't find Truly. When she didn't meet us when we got home, I figured she was sleeping in my room. She isn't there." I clutched my aunt's shoulders. "If something happened to her—"

"Settle down." Aunt Eunice removed my hands and turned a slow circle. "Let's try the shed. She could be locked in there."

"But why isn't she barking?" I feared the answer and sprinted for the shed.

Whimpers came through the dark yawning door of the shed. Faint, barely discernible, but there. "Truly." I reached for the chain to switch on the light. Nothing.

Stumbling, running into unseen obstacles, I searched with my hands held in front of me. The whines came from my right, and I turned. *There.* My hands encountered her squirming body, and using my fingers, I pulled the muzzle from her mouth and started to work on the bindings around her legs.

Truly whimpered louder. Her squirms made it difficult for my fingers to untie the knots. I scooped her into my arms. "I found her."

"Is she all right?"

I nodded. "I think so. I can't get the ties off. She's squirming too much."

Once in the house, I laid the yelping dog on the

kitchen table, against my aunt's protests that it wasn't a place for animals. I held my hand out, palm up. "Scissors, please."

The zip ties snipped quickly. As I worked, Truly whined. My heart ached with each whimper.

Once I had the dog free, Truly leaped for my face, covering me with kisses. I giggled and pushed her down. "What's this?" I lowered my head for a closer look.

A slip of paper stuck out from under Truly's collar. I pulled the paper free and read: *I want the rest of my money. I'll be in contact. Cooperate, and no one gets hurt.*

The blood drained from my face. "But I don't have any money." I handed the paper to Aunt Eunice. "I told you someone thinks there's something else here."

My aunt's eyes widened as she read. "What do we do if we can't find it? If this person," she waved the paper, "can't find something they hid themselves, how are we supposed to find it?"

I placed the dog on the floor. "I'd like to know how this person knows what we gave the police."

"Joe will be here in a few minutes." Uncle Roy walked into the room and bent to pet the jumping dog. "What are y'all doing?"

"First we needed to find the dog. Then we found a note tied around her collar demanding money." Aunt Eunice folded her arms across her chest. "Where have you been?"

"The dog was missing?" Uncle Roy straightened. "I was checking the other rooms of the house. We must have surprised the intruder, 'cause Summer's room is the only one destroyed. What money?"

I handed him the note. "Where have we not looked?

Is it possible someone else knew the money was here and took it?"

"It's possible. They at least knew the diamonds were beneath a rosebush."

Gravel crunched in the driveway out front, and Uncle Roy moved to open the door. By the time Aunt Eunice and I had sat at the table, Joe entered the room, followed by Uncle Roy and another officer.

"More excitement, Summer? I'm supposed to be watching a movie at April's. Can't you let me have one night without you getting into trouble?" Joe stood with legs apart. The other officer carried a pad of paper. "Officer White will take notes."

I leaned my elbow on the table and rested my weary head in the palm of my hand. "Someone broke into our house, tied up the dog in the shed with a note around her collar, and trashed my room. How's that for excitement?"

"A note?"

I handed him the slip of paper.

"You touched it? Please tell me you didn't."

"How else would I read the note?"

Joe's mouth set in a firm line. A muscle ticked in his jaw. His face remained impassive as he read it. "This sounds serious, Summer. You've managed to make an enemy."

"Who has an enemy?" Ethan stepped into the room, and I straightened in my chair. He came. Because he'd heard we had more trouble? *Dare I hope?*

I used my hand, attempting to smooth my hair. I glanced at my clothes. *Horror.* I hadn't had time to change and still wore dirt-covered shorts and a T-shirt. *Why can't I ever look nice around Ethan?*

"You might as well read it, too. Everyone else has touched and read it." Joe handed the note to Ethan.

A muscle clenched in Ethan's jaw as he clamped his lips together. His look hardened. "This is getting serious. Any idea who this could be?"

Joe shook his head. "I considered Nate, being as he's the newcomer and all, but he was at the picnic the whole time. I can attest to the fact. Can you think of anyone who wasn't there? I'm thinking our diamond culprit has an accomplice."

"Most of the church was there. Maybe a few more."

Aunt Eunice popped up from her seat. "I'll make coffee. Looks like this is going to be a long night. Joe, can you take a look at Summer's room while the coffee's brewing?"

"Someone was in your room?" Ethan turned his gaze on me.

"Tore. It. Up." Uncle Roy lowered his bulk into the chair my aunt had vacated. "Pillows, mattress, everything. Gone. Worthless. De—"

"They get it, Uncle Roy." Boy, how that man could go on. "Someone thinks I've got something that belongs to them. They'll figure out I don't, and that'll be the end of that."

"Don't be flippant about this, Summer. This is getting dangerous." Ethan slapped a hand on the table. "Just like I said it would."

I stood and stared him down. "Well, I haven't done anything in days. I haven't pounded the pavement. I haven't interviewed witnesses. I haven't been on a stakeout. I haven't—"

"A stakeout?" Ethan ran a hand through his hair.

"Are you serious? Joe, are you listening to this?"

"I'm listening." Joe placed a restraining hand on Ethan's shoulder. "Ethan, Summer is going to do what Summer wants to do. Haven't you figured that out yet? I'm keeping an eye on her. She hasn't been putting herself in harm's way. If she does, I'll throw her in jail."

"No, but harm seems to be finding her." Ethan rubbed his face with both hands. "I'm tired. I can't think straight." He raised his head and pierced me with his gaze. "Is the coffee finished, Aunt Eunice?"

"It sure is." She plopped mugs on the table in front of us and started pouring the dark, steaming liquid. "Sugar and cream are on the table. Do you want a pad of paper and something to write with?"

Joe lowered the mug he'd lifted to his lips. "For what?"

"Brainstorming." Aunt Eunice set the pot on the ceramic trivet in the center of the table. "We're all here, so we might as well help you crack this thing."

"Eunice." Joe looked worried, the poor dear. I snorted behind my mug. He turned to glare at me. "I can't have you all involved in a police investigation."

"We're already involved," I pointed out. "My dog was tied up, my room was trashed, and—"

"I know, Summer. You got a note. This is all the more reason why you need to stay out of the way and let me do my job." He rubbed a hand across his face. "You're my cousin. I care more than I should about this case. And you're frustrating me to no end!"

Aunt Eunice plopped a yellow legal pad in front of Joe, who rolled his eyes and slumped in his chair. "I've got my own." He pulled a small tablet from his pocket.

"But this pad is bigger. You can take more notes."

"I give up." Joe rested his chin in his hand.

"Okay. We know this much." I held up my fingers one at a time to separate my points. "One, there's more money hidden somewhere on this property, or at least someone thinks there is. Two, the suspect seems to have help or is very confused." I glanced at the empty pad in the other officer's hand. "Why aren't you taking notes?

"Three, they'll be contacting me again, and four, I have no idea where to look.

"And we found millions of dollars' worth of diamonds, cash hidden in a rusty can—that one still boggles my mind—and a bloody gardening glove." I put my right hand to my head. "Oh, wait—make that one pair of coveralls, two gardening gloves, and a dead body." I folded my hands on the table in front of me. "What can you add to this investigation, Joe? Have you tried matching the blood on the glove to the murdered stranger?"

"Summer, I'm warning you. I know how to do my job, and it doesn't include discussing every aspect of this case with you. Besides, I'm asking to be released from this case. It's a huge conflict of interest."

"That's great," I said. "You can help me solve it without all the legal mumbo jumbo."

Loud voices drifted on the nighttime breeze, carrying shrieks and curses. Joe's hand flew to the weapon on his hip, and followed closely by Ethan, he burst out the back door toward the woods. I didn't know what Ethan could do, considering he was unarmed, but admiration washed over me for him going with my cousin into what could possibly be a dangerous situation.

Uncle Roy rose from the table. "I'll get my gun."

Truly shot out behind them, barking with such intensity that her body shook. Not wanting her to leave us behind, Aunt Eunice and I followed, armed with knives from the butcher block on the counter.

We looked like rednecked clichés.

Uncle Roy arrived, panting. The rest of us stood in a circle, our backs to each other, staring into the dark woods around us. Poor Cousin Joe seemed on the verge of tears—probably at the sight of us armed with kitchen utensils and stomping around his prospective crime scene.

I clamped a hand over my mouth to stifle a giggle. Joe glared and threw his hands in the air. "I give up. If there was somebody here, they're gone now. Along with any evidence they may have left behind."

"There was somebody here, Joe." I lowered my knife, only to have it snatched by my cousin. He moved to disarm Aunt Eunice.

"Yeah, but y'all made so much noise following me, you've scared them off." He held out his hand for Uncle Roy's gun. "The only person I invited was Ethan, and he's the only one not running off half-cocked."

Ethan stood with his legs spread shoulder width apart. He moved out of our circle and shrugged.

"Y'all stay still. Let me take a look around." Joe pulled a small pen-sized flashlight from his pocket. A twinge of envy crept in. I wanted one. It would go great in my investigative pack. Much better than the bulky kind Aunt Eunice kept in the kitchen cabinet. I wondered whether Joe could get me one.

He shone his light around the small clearing. "Here we go."

Despite his orders, I stepped next to him. Two

distinct sets of footprints were visible in the soft ground. One set larger than the other. "There were two people here. My guess, a man and a woman. Could be a domestic disturbance."

Joe glanced at me as if I were capable of writing a *Dolt* book of my own. "I can see that, Sherlock."

"Miss Marple."

"Excuse me?"

"You called me Sherlock. I prefer Miss Marple. No comparison in age, though. I also answer to Nancy Drew."

"Summer—"

"Sorry." I stepped away from him. Maybe he could teach me something after all.

"The prints lead off into the bushes." Joe followed them, talking to himself. "And disappear right here." He turned back to us. "There's too much ground to cover in these woods. The prints are gone."

I wished Truly was a hound dog. One with a great sniffer.

Joe faced us. "Might as well head back to the house."

The trees were thick overhead and backlit by a full moon to where they resembled bushy arms reaching toward the heavens. What could someone be looking for out here? We rarely ventured this far into the woods. Not since childhood anyway. I skipped to catch up with the others.

Once inside, Aunt Eunice poured more coffee. I couldn't help but glance at my watch. *1:00! Horror.* I had to open the store in six hours.

"Someplace you need to be, Summer?" Joe returned

the knives to their block, handed Uncle Roy his rifle, then slipped his pistol in the shoulder holster he wore over his polo shirt.

"Not yet." I pulled up a chair and slouched on the hard wood.

"Summer, Roy, Eunice." Joe crossed his arms. "I want the three of you to find somewhere else to stay for a while."

Uncle Roy slammed a fist on the table. I jerked. "I won't be run out of my own home!"

"It isn't safe here, Uncle Roy."

"Don't use your patronizing tone with me, boy." Uncle Roy's face became the color of a ripe turnip. A sure sign of an escalating temper.

"Why don't you take me seriously?" Joe's face showed the beginning signs of redness. "If not for the fact that I'm an officer of the law, then because I'm family."

"It ain't that." Uncle Roy took a deep breath. "I'm not going to run scared from my house, and that's final."

"I could order it."

"No, you can't, and don't threaten me, boy. I can still take you down."

At his comment, a giggle escaped me. The vision of roly-poly Uncle Roy taking down muscular, burly Joe did me in. The two men turned to glare at me.

"I'm requesting a transfer." Joe folded his arms. "I can't work in the same town my family lives in."

He'd been making that threat for years. I held up a hand to ward off his words. "Sorry. Just tired." I snorted.

"I'll stay, Joe." Ethan crossed his arms. "There's room for me on the sofa. If anything happens, you'll be the first I call."

Joe nodded.

"That's settled then." Aunt Eunice walked around the table collecting the full coffee mugs. "We're all tired. We're getting testy. Let's go to bed."

Sleep sounded good. But once everyone left and I crawled between the sheets spread over the pile of quilts covering my ripped mattress, my mind raced like a thoroughbred. *My hideaway. The old tree house.* I threw off the covers and slung my legs over the side. No time like the present.

I pulled on a pair of jean shorts under my T-shirt and headed to the kitchen to hunt up a flashlight. Once I'd found one, I eased open the back door. Ethan sat on the top step.

"Figured you'd be out soon." He held up a flashlight. "I wondered what took you so long to think of it."

"You did, huh? Must think you know me pretty well."

"I do." He held out his hand, and I took it. Did Ethan wonder how his tender gestures affected me?

The simple touch thrilled me. Tingles ran up my arm. My heart raced. If only he loved me as much as I loved him. "The tree house?"

"Yep." He pulled me along after him.

"Why didn't you call Joe?"

Ethan shrugged. "I honestly don't know. I thought you might be up for an adventure. A quick peek at our favorite childhood hangout. It's our special place. If we find anything, we'll let Joe know."

We walked the rest of the way in silence. I couldn't help but compare the way my hand felt engulfed in Ethan's. While Nate's hands were as smooth as mine,

Ethan's woodworking job gave him calluses. His hands were larger than Nate's, too. I felt safe. I gave his hand a squeeze and smiled when he returned it.

Once we stood under the tree house, Ethan shone the flashlight beam up the trunk of the massive oak. "I'll go first in case the ladder isn't steady. This wood has gotten too old."

"Okay." The "ladder" consisted of wooden planks nailed into the tree trunk. I was more than happy to let him go first.

He climbed as quick as a monkey and stood on the platform to wave me up. I grasped a plank above my head and began my ascent.

Halfway, the plank under my feet gave way. I reached for Ethan at the same instant he grabbed my wrist.

My gaze locked with his.

I tore mine away, trembling as I looked down. The ground seemed hundreds of feet away.

"Look at me, Summer. Keep your eyes on me. I'll pull you up."

"I can't." I forgot to breathe. My head was light. The ground spun below me.

"Yes, you can. Look at me."

My legs flailed as I searched for another anchor. *Lord, help me. I don't want to fall.*

"Remember, Tinkerbell can fly." Ethan's soft words drifted to me.

"I'm not Tinkerbell." My heart beat in my ears, threatening to drown out all other sound.

"You're my Tinkerbell."

I came to my senses and allowed him to pull me up. I lay on the rough wood to catch my breath, focusing on

Ethan's face. He smiled.

"You all right?"

I nodded and pushed to a sitting position.

"Great." He shone his light around the dilapidated structure, pointing out nooks and crannies my uncle had built to supply me with hiding places for my treasures.

There. In the eaves. A box I'd never placed there when I was a child. "Up there, Ethan." I pointed. A pine box, glowing white in the moonlight with its newness.

He reached up and stopped. After yanking his T-shirt over his head, Ethan wrapped it around the box, pulled it from its perch, and lifted the lid. He whistled. "Bingo." Ethan handed the wrapped box to me.

Inside, rolled in neat little bundles, were many crisp bills.

"That's a lot of money. A lot more than what we found in that rusty can."

"About that can." Ethan lowered the lid on the pine box. "The can was your aunt and uncle's cruise money."

"What? Then, how—" I wrapped my arms around my knees.

Ethan lowered himself to the floor beside me.

"I buried the can on your uncle's say-so. He claimed it back from Joe the same day. He said if he didn't hide it, Eunice would spend it. When I buried the can, there weren't any diamonds in the hole. Summer, your aunt's been talking about her cruise money all over town. My guess is that somebody heard her, saw the freshly dug hole, and decided to take advantage of it. They most likely planned on retrieving it quickly, but then you three returned from vacation."

"I really stink at this investigating stuff." Sadness

slumped my shoulders. I really thought I had what it took to solve this case. Instead, the web of intrigue became more complicated. Why would someone send me a note requesting something I had if they hid it up here? Could there be more than one person after this cash?

"Don't take it too hard." He laid a hand on my shoulder. "No one in Mountain Shadows can figure out your aunt and uncle. God broke the mold when He made that pair."

"Thank goodness." I rested my chin on my knees, striving to keep my gaze averted from his well-muscled chest. Here we were, alone in the dark. Was Ethan dense, or didn't he care? *God help me.* Thankful for the night to hide the tears welling in my eyes, I forced my voice to remain steady. "But why didn't the crook hide the diamonds and the cash together?"

"Not enough room. It seems to me there are at least two people working against each other. Whoever hid them didn't want the other to know where both the diamonds and the cash were."

"Now what?"

"We turn the money over to Joe." Ethan stood and offered me a hand up.

"What do I do when they come for it?"

"We'll cross that bridge when we get there."

"I don't want to end up like that dead boy." I stood and stared through the trapdoor at something much scarier. "I can't get back down."

"Sure you can. I'll go first. Right in front of you. Just follow me."

The idea sounded good, but reinjuring my ankle and limping for three days didn't appeal to me. "I'll stay here.

You get the ladder."

"Summer, I'm not lugging the ladder all the way out here."

"Then tell Uncle Roy to do it." I refused to climb down the tree.

"You are the most exasperating woman." I could tell from his smile he liked the verbal sparring.

"And you are the most stubborn man." I returned the smile.

Ethan laughed. "Okay, we both take the prize. Trust me, Tink. I won't let you fall. You can ride piggy back if you want."

"As if." That's all I needed. To be plastered against him. I sighed. "I'll follow you."

The climb down scared me more than coming up, if that were possible. My legs shook so severely, I missed a rung and scraped the shin of my right leg. If I'd been a cursing woman, the birds would've flown from the trees with the severity of my words. Instead, I hissed against the pain.

When I reached the broken board, I fished around with my leg, searching for the next rung. My legs weren't long enough. Before I knew it, I was flying. With one arm around my waist, Ethan swung me around until I clutched the tree, my legs on the lower plank of wood.

"A little warning would be nice." I clasped a hand to my chest. "I almost had a heart attack."

He laughed. "Good thing you don't weigh much."

"Yeah. Good thing." I closed my hands and sagged against the tree. The bark felt rough beneath my cheek. I had a deep, abiding love for the tree and would never leave it.

"Come on, Summer."

With a sigh, I inched my way down. When I'd made it to the bottom, I had an overwhelming urge to kiss the ground. My new best friend. I glanced above us.

"Won't the thieves notice the broken plank when they come for their money?"

"They sure will." Ethan looked up, hands resting on his hips. "I'll dig around for a weathered piece of wood and replace it later today."

I pushed the button on my watch to illuminate the face. *3:00.* The problem with owning your own business was you couldn't call in sick. All I'd get was a couple hours of sleep. I'd rather spend it with Ethan. "Too late to go to bed now. How about I fix us some breakfast?"

"Sounds good to me." Ethan flung an arm over my shoulders, and we walked to the house.

While he stared at the pine box sitting in front of him on the kitchen table, I whipped up some ham and cheese omelets. My eyes were gritty from lack of sleep. I'd never thought almost-thirty would be too old for all-nighters, but I'd been wrong before.

When I turned around, Ethan had redonned his T-shirt and held my suspect notebook I'd left on the table. I wanted to kick myself.

"What's this?"

I set his plate in front of him. "My suspect list."

"Why's Terri Lee at the top?"

"She's my number one." I sat down, my own plate before me.

"Why?"

"I don't trust her."

"Why?"

"Can't you say anything else?" I lifted my fork then set it down. "She's shifty."

"She is not."

"She is, and she's the likely culprit. She designs her own jewelry and wants or needs more diamonds." I pointed a finger at him.

"Why are Mabel and Ruby here? And Duane Parker? Don't tell me you put him on the list because he just got out of prison. That wouldn't be fair." He frowned and peered closer at the list. "And Nate's on here then crossed off."

"Ruby turned up with diamond jewelry that looks like it's worth a fortune, and Mabel has a brand-new Cadillac. Where'd they get the money? Huh?" I picked up my fork, stabbed my omelet, and stuffed a bite in my mouth. I didn't speak it, but I'd taken Nate off because he hung around me so much he'd have difficulty getting into trouble.

"How does your aunt feel about having her friends on this list?"

"She told me to ask God who should go on it."

"Did you?"

"Not yet. But I will. As soon as I get the chance. I'm sorry if I suspect your girlfriend, but—"

"She isn't my girlfriend." Ethan's frown deepened, his brows almost meeting between his eyes.

"But y'all went on a date."

He looked taken aback. "We never went on a date. Who told you that?"

"Terri Lee. She said y'all went to dinner the other night."

"That's not true."

"See, Ethan, she's guilty. Why would she lie about something like going out to dinner?" I knew the answer to the question. I just wanted to know whether he did.

"I don't know, but I'll ask her. I've known you since the summer you turned ten. If I were to date someone, don't you think I'd tell you?" He grabbed my hand, said a quick blessing over his breakfast, and dug into his omelet like a man who hadn't eaten in a week. When he finished, he dropped his fork with a clatter and stood, clutching the box.

He looked at me with wounded eyes. "You're my best friend, Summer. I wouldn't leave you out on something as important as who I'm dating."

Ouch. I'm sorry. I couldn't stand gazing at the hurt on his face. I wanted so much more than friendship. Guilt over not telling Ethan about Nate flooded through me. I opened my mouth to confess then closed it. I'd pick a better time. When he was in a good mood.

"See you later. Thanks for breakfast." And he left, leaving the pine box on the table.

I pushed aside the uneaten portion. I wasn't hungry. My heart sat in my chest like a cold, hard stone. I wanted to take it out and bash myself in the head. Instead, I grabbed the box and shoved it in the pantry. Joe would be livid, but someone wanted something from me. I intended to give it to them.

I didn't know why Terri Lee wanted to play games, but I intended to find out. During my lunch break, I'd pay another visit to the jeweler.

Aunt Eunice and I moved around the candy store as if we wore weighted shackles. We didn't get the batch of peanut brittle mixed fast enough, and the whole place smelled like burned peanuts. I almost cried when we dumped the ruined candy in the garbage. For the first time since the store opened, I thanked God we didn't have many customers.

After work Aunt Eunice went home, and despite my exhaustion, I dragged myself down the street to the jewelers.

The same snotty, chubby Cruella de Vil lady stood behind the counter, looking down her nose. "I'd like to speak with Terri Lee, please."

"She isn't in." The woman actually had the audacity to turn her back on me.

"Do you know when she'll return?"

"She doesn't work today."

"Excuse me." I reached across the counter and tapped her shoulder. "Can you give me her home address? It's very important."

The woman gave me a long-suffering sigh. "We're not allowed to give out that information. But if you see her, tell her she's fired."

Okay. She dismissed me, but why wasn't Terri Lee working? Both times I'd visited the jewelers, Terri Lee happened to be out. I left the store.

Did Terri Lee still live with her parents? Had she gotten her own apartment? I wished I'd asked Ethan where she lived. Dating or not, I was certain he'd know. But first I needed a nap.

12

I didn't make it to the Ruperts' until the next afternoon. My lack of rest caught up with me. I napped through the night and into morning.

The Ruperts lived five miles out of town on a dirt road badly in need of grading. My head and joints ached after bouncing my way down the rutted street.

I stopped in front of a small ranch-style house. Peeling gray or weathered white paint, it was hard to tell, covered the wooden panels. One glance at the roof told me it most likely leaked. I'd forgotten Terri Lee came from such humble beginnings. You'd never know from the expensive clothes she wore. I guessed she regularly drove two hours to the outlet mall. Anything for appearances.

Two red bloodhounds met me, slobbering and barking. I pressed on the horn until a heavyset woman stepped onto the porch. Terri Lee's mother. She'd been a beautiful woman once, but hard times had left their mark, streaking ebony hair with silver and lining her once smooth, high cheekbones with wrinkles. She had heavy-lidded, faded dark eyes. Same as Terri Lee's. What some called bedroom eyes.

She yelled for the dogs to quiet down and used a few more words I wouldn't repeat before the hounds slunk away and I could get out of my car. Mrs. Rupert didn't smile a welcome, nor did she come off the porch to greet me.

I advanced toward her, my hand extended. "Mrs. Rupert? You probably don't remember me, but I went to school a couple of years behind Terri Lee."

"I remember you." She didn't return my handshake, and I let my hand fall. "What do you want? I hope you ain't here drumming up business for that candy store of yours. I'm diabetic."

"We have sugar-free." I shook my head. "But that isn't why I'm here. Is Terri Lee home?"

"Ain't been home all night. Don't know where she's at."

Nor do you care, from the way you're acting. "Does she have a place in town where she stays once in a while?"

Mrs. Rupert laughed. A high, shrill cackle. "That girl don't make enough money to live in town. You're a regular comedian."

Okay. People had called me lots of things before, but never a comedian. I don't think she meant it as a compliment. "So, she doesn't earn a decent salary at the jewelers?"

"Oh, you mean with her jewelry? She sells a few pieces here and there, but she usually gets her stuff from men, if you know what I mean."

Mrs. Rupert eased herself into a rickety rocker without offering me a seat. "She brought that boy out here, and he turned up dead. Didn't seem to break her heart none. Right away, she's started chasing after that handsome greeter at the church." Mrs. Rupert snorted. "Like he'd give her type the time of day. And I've heard she's been seen with that convict. The one who wanders the highway at night. Freaky."

I shifted from one foot to the other, eyeing the two hounds sneaking back around the corner of the house. "Mr. Banning treats everyone the same, Mrs. Rupert. With respect, kindness, and God's grace. As for Duane. . ."

"Well, he'd better run as hard and fast from Terri Lee

as possible. She ain't nothin' but trouble, that one." Mrs. Rupert rocked her chair with such force that I expected her to take flight.

The rest of the conversation went nowhere fast. The direction it headed made me downright uncomfortable. I didn't count myself as one of Terri Lee's fans, but I hadn't counted on such negativity from her mother. It made me determined to find out why Terri Lee lied about dating Ethan.

"Thank you for your time, Mrs. Rupert." I started to offer my hand again, but remembering her nonacceptance earlier, instead wiped the palm down my pant leg to hide my intentions. I headed toward my car, keeping my eyes on the dogs.

"I'll tell her you came by. Don't know if she'll be happy about it or not."

Mrs. Rupert remained in the rocker while I backed the car down the drive. Her unblinking stare made me nervous, and I kept glancing from my rearview mirror to anywhere but her face. The dashboard, the trees around her property, my rearview mirror.

My rearview mirror! I slammed on the brakes in time to avoid backing into Joe's squad car. My cousin pursed his lips and shook his head at me. My heart pounded so hard I swore it would soon be beating outside my body.

Joe strode to my window. "Summer, you need to watch where you're going."

"What are you doing here? My heart stopped, and I think I died for about two seconds. I swear I did."

"I could ask you the same thing. Why are *you* here?"

I couldn't read his expression behind his mirrored

black sunglasses. He pressed his lips into a thin line. "I need Mrs. Rupert to identify a body."

I flung the door open faster than I could say, "Where's the corpse?" and jogged after Joe. "Why do you need Mrs. Rupert? Did you know Terri Lee's missing? Is it her?"

Joe stopped and turned to face me. "You know I can't divulge that information, Summer. Why do you bother to ask? Do you enjoy hearing me say no?"

"Just in case." I shrugged.

"Go home."

I stopped and crossed my arms, pouting. Why did he insist on treating me like his younger cousin? I happened to be, but I didn't like that he treated me that way.

Joe approached the porch where Mrs. Rupert still rocked. He stalked past the barking dogs as if they were noisy Chihuahuas not worthy of his attention. He spoke in a low voice, and Mrs. Rupert's hand flew to her chest. She nodded then followed Joe. Neither of them looked at me as they passed.

I slid into my car and slammed it into drive, not wanting them to leave me behind. The dogs yelped and leaped out of my way as I turned a wide circle in the yard and sped after them.

A half hour later, I pulled into the parking lot of the Mountain Shadows' funeral home and makeshift morgue. Sometimes they held bodies at the clinic.

Joe kept a hand on Mrs. Rupert's elbow as he steered her inside. I tried to follow but halted at a stern look from Joe. Fine. I'd wait outside. The funeral home had a wonderful rose garden complete with wrought iron benches, and I settled on one to wait.

I didn't wait long. From the relieved look on Mrs. Rupert's face, the body couldn't be Terri Lee's. For the first time that afternoon, I'd seen the woman smile. I popped off the bench like a demented jack-in-the-box.

"Joe?"

"It's Doris Ingram. From the jewelers." He held the squad car door open for Mrs. Rupert.

"How'd she die? Why'd you have Mrs. Rupert identify her?"

I swear my cousin held the monopoly on long-suffering sighs as he turned to me. He let out a good one before he answered. "I'm not at liberty to say how she died, Summer. And the Ruperts are the only family she has. Doris and Mrs. Ingram are second cousins."

Mrs. Rupert leaned out the window. "Someone strangled her. I saw the marks on her neck with my own eyes."

Strangled? I froze in my tracks. We had a young man dead by stab wounds and a woman strangled. Were the deaths related? Different deaths. Different ways of dying. Where was Terri Lee? Did she kill one or both of these people? Was she lying dead somewhere? Could there be a murderer in Mountain Shadows I didn't suspect yet?

My heart ached for the dead woman. Left with no family to know or care if she was dead or alive. She hadn't been the friendliest person, but I vowed to attend her funeral even if I'd be the only one there.

"When's the funeral?" I called out.

"Won't be one," Joe called out his window. "Once the medical examiner is finished with the body, she'll be cremated and put to rest here at the home.

"Oh, and tell Aunt Eunice to set two extra plates

for dinner. I'm coming over to confiscate what you and Ethan found. I'll be bringing April."

I stomped my foot. Ethan told on me. Now I'd have no leverage against the crooks. Was there nothing sacred between friends?

"Summer? Everything okay?" Nate strolled toward me. "What are you doing at the funeral home?"

"Seeing an old friend." My gaze followed Joe's car from the parking lot. He steered back toward the Ruperts' house.

"It's great running into you." Nate leaned forward for a kiss, only connecting with my cheek as I turned my head. "I hoped we could get together tonight."

"I can't. My aunt's having people over for dinner."

"Great. I'm free. What time?"

What time? I turned to stare at him. Did he invite himself over? From the smile on his face, I'd say he'd done just that. I thought about telling him no but caved. I was too tired to argue. "Oh. Uh. Okay. Five o'clock?"

"Great. I'll be a little late." Another misplaced kiss and Nate went on his way.

I glanced at my watch. Aunt Eunice would be angry if I was late for dinner. With constant glances in my rearview mirror, I sped home.

Aunt Eunice cast me a cold look over her shoulder when I entered the kitchen and started mashing potatoes.

"Sorry I'm late. I visited Mrs. Rupert."

"Why? You never hung out there when you were younger."

"Just some questions I hoped she could answer." Aunt Eunice frowned at my evasiveness. I couldn't tell her I wanted to confront Terri Lee about saying she was dating Ethan. That would set the conversation off in a direction I didn't want to go. Thankfully, Aunt Eunice took the hint.

"How is Mrs. Rupert?"

"Not very friendly." *To put it mildly.* I lit the burner on the gas stove. "Joe showed up as I was leaving. Seems he needed Mrs. Rupert to identify a body."

That got my aunt's attention. She loosened her folded arms and dropped them to her sides. "Who was it? Terri Lee?"

"No. Doris Ingram, but Terri Lee hadn't been home all night. Her mother doesn't know where she is. Oh, and Joe, April, Ethan, and Nate are coming for dinner."

"How tragic about Doris. I didn't know the woman well, but—" She turned back to her work. "Why is Nate coming?"

"Your fine cooking."

"Don't hogwash me." The arms folded again.

I imitated one of my cousin's sighs then spewed out the information. "Last night Ethan and I found a box of money. Hidden in my old tree house." I dumped freshly snapped beans into a pan. "Joe's coming over tonight to retrieve it, and he's bringing April. Nate invited himself."

Aunt Eunice paused. "We can't talk about the case with him here. He's not family."

"Neither are Ethan or April."

"They might as well be. At least Ethan is involved. He's the one who found the diamonds, after all." She went back to her work. "I'd better make a bigger meat loaf. If I were you, I'd try to butter up your cousin somehow. He's going to be mad you didn't call him right away. Why didn't you?"

"Ethan was going to, but he left in a huff. I'd hoped he forget about the box."

~~~

Joe whistled between his teeth when he lifted the lid on the box. "There's got to be tens of thousands of dollars in here."

"Before I called you, I debated about whether or not I should turn it in." Ethan held up a hand when Joe opened his mouth to protest. "I know, but Summer wondered what she'd do when the thief discovers it's missing. Obviously, we're dealing with more than one, and they're playing against each other. I tend to agree with her."

"Regardless, Ethan. We have to obey—" The ringing of the doorbell interrupted Joe.

"That'll be Nate." I rose from my chair.

"Summer." Joe reached out to stop me. "Not that it's any of my business, but don't go getting too involved with Nate. You don't know anything about him, and he's new to town."

I snatched my arm away. "I can take care of myself. Instead of focusing on one person, you ought to be investigating everyone in this town."

"I am. Everyone on the list you made. Aunt Eunice told me—"

"Good grief, Joe. At least you're doing something."

The door bell rang again.

"Hide the money." Aunt Eunice snatched the box from the table and stashed it in the pantry.

"Fingerprints, Aunt Eunice." Joe grabbed a nearby dish

towel and wrapped it around the box before pulling it from the shelf. "I'm running this to the station. Officer Wayne is going to be helping quite a bit with the investigation. Be back in half an hour." He planted a kiss on April's forehead then disappeared out the back door.

I left the kitchen and dragged my feet to the front door. You'd think I'd be more excited about having male company. Maybe it was the company. I would have to find a way to discourage Nate's attention, regardless of my wisecrack to Joe. Nate didn't cause my heart to beat faster. No violins played. No waves crashed. Aunt Eunice would say my expectations were too high.

"Hello, Nate." I pushed open the door and turned my face, avoiding another of his kisses. What was with this man and kissing?

A frown crossed his face for the briefest second, which he replaced with a smile. "Smells good."

I led him into the kitchen and introduced him to everyone. He greeted Ethan, laid the charm on April thick enough to make my stomach queasy, and dismissed my aunt and uncle, which made my temper flare.

"Pull up a chair, young man," Uncle Roy told him, waving an arm to his right. "We're waiting for one more."

"I'll fix him a plate and keep it warm."

Aunt Eunice had prepared a feast. A four-pound meat loaf sat in the center of the table along with all the fixings.

"How do you like the church, Nate?" Aunt Eunice plopped a pile of mashed potatoes on his plate.

"The people are real friendly." Nate reached across the table for the salt. "I've been the blessed one." I handed out bowls for the salad.

"Would you have ketchup, by any chance?"

The rest of us froze and stared at Nate. None of us dared ask for ketchup while eating Aunt Eunice's meat loaf.

Aunt Eunice didn't say a word. Instead, with her nose in the air, she went to the pantry. She reached for the shelf above her head. Things happened in slow motion as her elbow hit the can containing her cruise money. The can fell to the floor, spilling bills across the linoleum.

"That's a lot of dough," Nate remarked, his eyes wide.

"Uh, it's our cruise money." Aunt Eunice dropped to her knees and scooped the cash into her apron. I wished for a larger house. One with a formal dining area where we couldn't view the pantry from our dinner table.

Joe entered to the sight of Aunt Eunice rising from the floor with her apron full of money. His face turned such a bright shade of red that I feared for his heart. It must be difficult trying to be an upstanding lawman in a family like ours. He'd warned my aunt and uncle many times to keep their money in the bank.

Ethan and April sat frozen. April's lips twitched as she managed to control herself. A muscle ticked in Ethan's jaw. Uncle Roy sat silent, his mouth opening and closing like a beached fish.

A fit of the giggles overtook me. Soon I was snorting and trying to control myself. "Sorry. Sorry." I fell into a chair. Only in the Meadows home would something this absurd happen.

Nate took another bite of his ketchup-covered meat loaf, chewed, and swallowed. "What did y'all do? Rob a bank?"

13

Aunt Eunice stood, her hands gathering the apron around the cash. "Oh, you. You're such a funny guy. Rob a bank, indeed." She elbowed me in the back of the head as she passed. The knock effectively halted my snorting. *Ouch!*

She dumped the money on the counter and tried stuffing it back in the can. Bills stuck out every which way, several floating like feathers to the kitchen floor. "It came out of the can; it should go back in."

"You've got to rubber-band it together." Uncle Roy joined her beside the sink. Several of the bills fluttered from the countertop and landed in the sudsy dishwater.

Joe looked close to tears by this point, and from the expression on Ethan's face, he'd be joining me in the snorting section. April hid her grinning face behind a napkin. Nate seemed frozen in shock. He still held a forkful of mashed potatoes halfway to his mouth.

"Stop it, Roy. Look what you're doing." Aunt Eunice slapped his hands.

"I can't take this anymore." Joe rose from the table and headed to the pantry. He emerged with a brown paper sack. "Excuse me." He pushed Eunice and Roy aside and scraped the cash into the sack, which he then deposited beneath his chair. "I'm putting this in the bank where it belongs. Can I eat now?"

"Gee, Joe, you act like this is the money you took to the po-lice station." Aunt Eunice frowned. "You can't tell us what to do with our own things." Aunt Eunice lowered her bulk back in her chair.

The redness increased in Joe's face as he sat down. "Next time anyone in this family finds any evidence, give it to me immediately. Night or day, I don't care. And please don't touch anything. I'm going to have to start arresting y'all for obstruction of justice and tampering with a crime scene. Do I make myself clear?"

The potatoes finally made it into Nate's mouth. He closed his eyes in an expression of ecstasy before swallowing. "I've got to admit. Coming here for dinner sure beats watching TV."

"Yeah, we're a regular riot." I poured sweetened iced tea into everyone's glasses. "Never a dull moment." I met Ethan's gaze across the table. He smiled and winked, sending a flood of warmth through me.

The bag beneath Joe's chair crackled whenever he moved his feet, the only sound during the remainder of dinner. Its presence made me uncomfortable, serving as a constant reminder that a crook and murderer ran the streets. I shook it off. The stolen cash, if that's what we'd found, sat at the police station, safely locked up. My aunt and uncle's cruise fund wasn't large enough to attract unwanted attention, was it?

Of course, the condition of my wrecked bedroom didn't help my nervousness. Someone had violated my personal space. I still hadn't had time to put it back in order, and stepping inside made me shiver.

After we finished eating, Ethan and I cleared off the table as we'd done numerous times over the years. Old habits die hard. My heart constricted as our hands brushed reaching for a stack of plates. My face flamed, and I jerked my hand back.

We usually chattered like a couple of magpies while I washed and he dried. I searched my brain for a safe topic of discussion. I didn't think "I love you" would suffice.

"Looks like you and Nate are getting serious." Ethan dried a dish and set it on the counter.

I shrugged. "Not really. I think he'd like it to be."

"And you?"

"I don't know." I glanced at him. "Why all the questions?"

"I miss our talks, Summer. We used to have such fun."

"We argued a lot."

"But it was fun arguing."

"What? You didn't enjoy our midnight tree climb?" I needed to steer the subject away from serious matters.

"Immensely. Felt like old times. Look." He turned to face me. "I knew if I waited too long, you'd. . . I mean you're not the type of—"

My heart stilled. I held my breath waiting for him to continue. Was he finally going to declare himself? Something I'd waited half my life for?

"Summer." Nate walked up behind us. "Would you like to take a walk?"

"Well, I, uh—" I wanted to wring Nate's neck. What had Ethan been about to say?

"Go ahead." Ethan took the dishrag from my hands. "I'll finish up here."

Nate clapped him on the shoulder. "Great." He grasped me by the elbow and almost pushed me out the back door.

"Hey. A little rough, Nate."

"Sorry." His hand fell to hold mine. "Isn't it beautiful out here? I wanted to share it with you."

What a lovely evening. The time when locusts sang

and fireflies flitted. Living on the outskirts of town, our road didn't have streetlamps, and it got really, really dark after sunset. I tilted my head, staring at the sky. The stars sparkled like the diamonds we'd found, complete with their own black velvet pouch.

"You've got stars in your eyes, Summer."

Oh brother. What a way to ruin a perfectly good evening. Somehow, mushy endearments sounded practiced when Nate spoke them.

"Show me where you and Ethan went last night."

That stopped me in my tracks. "Why?"

"Just curious. Exciting things are happening around here."

I strained to see his face, unable to make out his features. "You haven't been here long enough to know. Exciting things happen all the time."

"All small towns are the same. Are you going to show me or not?"

"I'll have to get a flashlight. It'll be impossible to see in those thick trees."

Nate released my hand long enough to pull a small keychain light from his pocket. "Always be prepared. That's my motto."

"Uh." I gnawed my lip, searching my mind for a new plan. "I still don't know why it's so important for you to see the tree house."

"Something to do. It'll be fun." He tugged at my hand.

Despite my misgivings, I led the sugar-talking Boy Scout through the woods to my tree house. "I spent a lot of time here as a child. Ethan and I were reliving old times."

"Really?" He muttered something else under his breath

I didn't catch. Nate shone the beam through the door. When he moved to climb the ladder, I stopped him.

"I wouldn't. The planks aren't very strong. I would have fallen if Ethan hadn't caught me."

"I would've saved you." Nate clicked off his flashlight. "I'd like to save you from this small-town life." His arms snaked around my middle and yanked me to him.

"You're too close." I pushed against his chest. His laughter rumbled.

"Stop being a tease, Summer." He twisted his hand in my hair. "You're asking for trouble. In more ways than one."

"Aren't you going up?" I said. My blood ran cold.

"Your prudish attitude's ruined the idea." He pulled me closer. "Why can't you and I have a little fun?"

Something told me he'd be returning on his own. My instincts told me I needed to get away from him. *Now.*

Nate released my hair and slung an arm around my shoulders. His lips stretched into a thin smile. "Are you ready to head to the house?"

I pulled away. "Not with you." And what did he mean, *asking for trouble*? I'd done nothing to lead him on. I've been the perfect picture of virtue. At least with him. My thoughts toward Ethan were something I'd been working on for years.

"Don't pout. It doesn't become you." Nate's voice sounded cold. He'd stopped his sweet-talking.

I turned and headed toward the kitchen's square of yellow light. Once I stepped into the safety of the open yard, I spun around to face Nate. "I don't think we should see each other anymore. You want something I'm not able to give."

"Summer," he said, "you're so irresistible I can't help myself."

"You'll learn." I spun on my heel and marched toward the house.

"It's Banning, isn't it?" His words cut through the night.

"Yes." I spoke so softly I wondered whether I'd said it aloud.

"You'll regret this, my dear."

I glanced over my shoulder. Nate melted into the shadows. From the front of the house came tuneless whistling as Duane took his walk. I stepped from the night into the warmth of Aunt Eunice's kitchen. Immediately the stress of walking with Nate dispelled, drifting on the wind.

Aunt Eunice wiped the speckled tabletop with a dishrag. The flab beneath her ample arms waved, and I smiled at the homey picture she made.

"Where's Ethan?" I locked the dead bolt behind me.

"He went home." Aunt Eunice tossed the rag into the sink. "Same as Joe and April. Your uncle's gone to bed. And I've just finished up in here." She reached behind her and untied her sunny yellow apron then tossed it across the back of a chair. "Follow me."

Uh-oh. I recognized her tone. Aunt Eunice had something that needed explaining. And usually I had the explaining to do.

I followed her into my messy bedroom. Aunt Eunice lifted the bed skirt and pulled out my book. "What's this? I thought I'd get started on putting your room back together, and I stumbled across it. *The Dolt's Complete Guide to Private Investigating*?"

"It's to help me solve this case." I snatched the book from her hand.

"Doesn't seem to be helping much. Unless you've got a suspect you haven't told anyone about."

"It will. I haven't had much of a chance to read."

I plopped on the edge of the bed and stared at the book. According to the cover, I could be a private investigator or at least be as smart as one. I read down the cover's listed points. Getting a license didn't interest me. I did want professional tips on gathering evidence. These case examples were interesting. I returned my gaze to my aunt's face. "I really want to solve this, Aunt Eunice. I'll take whatever help I can get."

The bed sagged beneath her weight. "It's going to be harder now that Joe is off the case. That other officer might throw you in the slammer for getting in the way."

Something inside me burned to follow these events through. Other than the candy store, I couldn't recall finishing a single thing I'd ever started. Flitting from one idea to another.

I shrugged. "I can't let it go now even if I wanted to. Someone thinks I have something I don't. If I back off the case, I don't think they'd leave me alone. I can do this. I know I can."

"I agree with your uncle on this one. It's not a game we're playing."

"I know that." I tossed the book back on my nightstand. "It's hard to explain. At first I thought it'd be fun trying to find out where the diamonds came from. Then everyone seemed so adamant I stay out of things. Now I don't feel I have a choice in the matter. It's either solve the case, or someone's going to do something bad. Maybe to me."

"I probably sound like I'm beating a dead horse here, but have you prayed about it? Asked God what you're supposed to do?" Aunt Eunice plucked a pillow from the floor. "About your safety and Ethan?"

"I don't even know where to start." Heaviness weighed me down. Tears pricked at my eyelids.

"Then you're in a bit of a pickle. But things sure would be easier if you didn't try relying on yourself all the time. God says His yoke is easy. His burden light. You should try asking Him sometime."

Aunt Eunice was right. But I'd done things my way for so long that I didn't know how to let go.

Truly joined my aunt and me on the bed, planting her sturdy body between us. I scratched behind her ear while my gaze roamed across the room. It resembled a war zone.

The curtains hung lopsided. Fingerprint powder covered every surface. Clothes hung from drawers or were scattered around the room. Stuffing from the mattress lay strewed about, and a metal spring poked my left buttock. At least I had a good reason to buy a new mattress—one of those pillow-top styles I've always wanted.

"I told Nate I didn't want to see him anymore." Saying the words gave me inner peace. Like an immense burden lifted from my shoulders.

"Any particular reason?"

"When I was with him, it was like avoiding the arms of an octopus. He suffocated me. Nate moved way too fast."

"He seemed like such a well-mannered boy." Aunt Eunice rose from the bed and scooped rumpled clothing into her arms.

"Nate seemed too perfect. Too well mannered and

smooth talking." *Give me a real man like Ethan any day.*

"Probably for the best." Aunt Eunice dropped the armload of clothes into the hamper. "You're hung up on Ethan anyway. It'll be hard to find someone who compares."

I rolled my eyes and plopped back on the bed. "I'm nothing but a little sister to him. His Tinkerbell."

She grabbed handfuls of mattress stuffing. "I think Ethan cares more than he lets on."

"You think so?" I sat upright. "He's just playing it cool? Hard to get?"

"He's still single, isn't he? A handsome young man like him." Aunt Eunice shoved an armful of stuffing at me. "You might want to stick this back in the mattress until you've got something better to sleep on."

Stuffing? Sleep? My aunt's views on Ethan's feelings were more important. "You think Ethan is single because he cares for me? Why doesn't he do something about it then? Make a move? Kiss me?" *Marry me.*

"Why don't you ask him?" She shoved the last wad at me. "Waste not, want not. It's late, and I'm going to bed." She cupped my cheek. "Either ask him, or wait to see what God does, huh?" Her fingers slid away, and she left the room.

Staring at the stuffing in my hands, I shook my head. I'd never heard of such a thing. *Restuffing a mattress?* Why wasn't everyone impulsive like me? If I wanted something, I went for it. The word *wait* wasn't in my vocabulary unless it meant confronting Ethan about his feelings for me.

My legs gave way beneath me, and I sank onto the mattress. It would be too mortifying to ask him and find out his feelings weren't the same as mine. I let go of the stuffing. It rolled from my open arms and fell in clumps back to the floor.

I groaned and followed the fluffy what-used-to-be-white stuff until my knees hit the floor. A sharp object pricked my knee, and I drew in my breath with a hiss. I glanced down. A trickle of blood welled and coursed down my shin. I pressed a handful of stuffing to the cut to halt the thin stream.

What did I cut myself on? My gaze traveled the room, halting at my nightstand. Where was the crystal vase I'd gotten for my birthday? Shards of glass glittered up from the fallen snow of the mattress stuffing reminding me of the diamonds.

I remembered something I'd read in my *Dolt's Guide*, and a smile spread across my face. Thieves always left something behind or took something with them. The crook's shoe might carry embedded pieces of broken glass. Now all I had to do was find the culprit and examine his footwear. Then I'd have my perpetrator.

I took fistfuls of the stuffing and shoved them into the mattress. My once-smooth bed became lumpy. Yep, I should've retired this mattress years ago. I shoved my arm through the hole in the fabric, struggling to even out the lumps.

Something stabbed me. A cry escaped, and I withdrew my hand, staring in revulsion at the slash across my palm. Pain throbbed through me. Blood dripped onto the wooden floorboards. Maybe I'd found the tool used to slash my mattress.

I held stuffing against the gash in my palm and headed to the bathroom, yelling as I passed my aunt and uncle's bedroom door. "I need some help!"

They both appeared, dressed in their pajamas. *Bless their hearts.* Uncle Roy held his gun.

"There's a knife in my mattress."

Aunt Eunice's maternal instinct kicked in when she saw the blood, and she rushed to me. She cradled my hand in her own. "This is going to take stitches. Roy, start the truck."

"I need to call Joe first." He chuckled. "Most of the time, people put the knife beneath the bed to cut the pains of labor. You aren't hiding something from us, are you?" He turned, his mouth split with a smile, and left the room.

"Yeah. Right." With my love life? I'd probably be childless and a spinster for my whole life. A person could always count on Uncle Roy to find a hillbilly fable to fit almost any circumstance.

"If you're going to call Joe, call him. Then get the truck started." Aunt Eunice clicked her tongue.

I pulled my hand from my aunt's. With the blood washed clean, what we'd thought was a gash looked more like a deep scratch. "I don't need stitches, Aunt Eunice. I need to clean and wrap my hand."

"I told you you'd get hurt messing with this case."

"I wasn't investigating. I was fixing my bed like you told me to." I yawned. *Too many late nights.* I stood like an obedient child while my aunt wrapped my hand. Finished, I went downstairs and lay prone on my back on the sofa. My hand throbbed, my knee stung, and my head ached. Pretty standard feelings for me this week.

Maybe twenty minutes later, Joe arrived entering the house with his own key. I didn't know Joe had a key to the house. I shrugged. Like Uncle Roy said, Joe might as well move in.

I remained where I lay, grunting a welcome as Joe marched past me. Minutes later, he returned, holding a plastic bag with what looked like a kitchen butcher knife inside.

"Ever seen this before?"

I shook my head. "It doesn't match our set." I sat up. "Could that be the knife that killed Terri Lee's friend? That guy they found dead in the woods? Will you be able to tell with my blood on it?"

Joe held up a hand to halt my questions. "It's quite possible, and, yes, we'll be able to determine if this was the knife used to kill David Young."

"Why would someone slash up my room then hide the incriminating evidence? They had to know we'd find it sooner or later. Do you think we could've interrupted whoever was in the house, and that's why they had to stash it so quickly?"

Joe glowered. "Incriminating evidence? Have you been reading again?"

—

After work on Friday, dressed with a new Band-Aid on my knee and fresh gauze wrapped around my hand, I drove the thirty miles to the nearest mattress outlet. My stomach soured. I'd slept with a knife inside my mattress, one possibly used to murder someone.

What if the killer had used the knife on me? I broke into a cold sweat. Life had definitely increased in excitement since finding the diamonds. This wasn't a story in a book, but real life. Things like this didn't happen in real life, did they?

The strip mall loomed in front of me, and I steered into the first available parking slot. I opened the door and slid from the driver's seat. Mabel's late-model black Cadillac was in the spot next to mine. Seeing that, I felt tempted to get back into mine and find another mattress dealer.

When I saw Mabel exiting the store, I ducked on the pretense of checking the bandage on my leg.

"Yoo-hoo!"

I grimaced and straightened. "Mabel, how are you?"

The woman wrapped me in a hug. "You sweet thing. Worrying about me. The question is, how are *you*? If someone attacked, stabbed me, I don't think I'd—"

"Wait a minute, Mabel." I pulled free of her suffocating grip and sickening sweet perfume. "Who told you someone stabbed me?"

"Well—" Mabel put her index finger to her lips. "I heard something about a knife, your bed, and you bleeding all over the house."

And the woman called herself a reporter. "But who were you talking to?"

"I don't remember. Somebody who spoke with somebody else, probably. It'll make a great story for the paper."

"I'm fine. I cut myself when I discovered the knife. Now, I intend to purchase a new mattress. Please don't mention anyone stabbing me and, whatever you do, don't write an article about it for the paper." I tossed the woman a quick smile to take the bite off my words and pushed open the door to the store.

Although I wasn't in Mountain Shadows, my reputation preceded me to the town of Oak Hollow. Every gaze in the store turned to me, and my face heated. An elderly man wearing a white tag with the name EDGAR in red ink took my arm and led me to a cushioned chair.

"Have a seat right here, darling. You tell us what you're looking for, and I'll see what kind of a deal I can get for you. My, the things you've had to endure." He shook his head as he patted my hand.

Something wasn't right. There was more going on than everyone thinking someone stabbed me, right? Complete strangers usually weren't this kind. I stared around the room in confusion. I wanted my aunt Eunice. I suddenly knew what a caged monkey felt like.

"Uh, I want one of your queen-size pillow-top mattresses. Not too expensive, please."

"You bet. Anything. Don't worry about the cost. The woman who left here told us all about what you've been through." With those words, the man turned and disappeared behind a door.

Horror. What had Mabel said? Things didn't get any clearer when the manager approached me. He clutched a clipboard in his right hand. "We're going to give you our top-of-the-line mattress for only a bit above cost."

I glanced up to meet his eyes. Were those tears?

"We want you to be as comfortable as possible."

"Sir." I stretched to see his name tag. "Mr. Miller. What exactly did she tell you?"

"How you'd tried recovering stolen diamonds and someone attacked you, and now you don't have much time left." He perched on the arm of the chair. "Honey, hasn't anyone told you?" The man hung his head. "No one should have to find out like this. From a stranger."

I choked back the giggles threatening to rise like

champagne bubbles. No wonder the Bible advised against gossip. "The last I heard, I'm in perfect health other than a skinned knee and a cut hand, Mr. Miller." I extended my palm. "I greatly appreciate your overwhelming generosity and Christian spirit, but I'll pay full price for the mattress if you'll deliver it for free."

The man tugged on his left earlobe. "Deal."

I left the store with a pink sales slip in my hand. I opened my car door, slid in, and then the laughter I'd held in check burst forth. I felt as if I'd played the childhood game of telephone, where what originally was said gets distorted as each person tells the next one. Aunt Eunice would get a kick out of this story.

The day's events kept me entertained on the half-hour drive back to Mountain Shadows. I'd call April as soon as I got home. We'd have a good laugh over the thought of me being at death's door.

Sobering, a question rose in my mind. What did Mabel mean when she said I didn't have much time? Could her statement be another part of the confusion, or did the reporter know something I didn't?

Worship and praise music blared from my car stereo. I opened my mouth to belt out the words to the song when my teethed clicked together from a sharp jolt. The seat belt jabbed into my clavicle.

Hey! Somebody had better have good automobile insurance. I glanced over my shoulder. A truck fender filled my back window. I pressed on the accelerator. The truck surged forward.

The truck rammed me again. My annoyance turned to fear. My knee connected with the steering wheel, bringing tears to my eyes.

Keeping one hand on the wheel, I fished in my purse for my cell phone and punched in number 1, Ethan's speed dial number.

No answer. I tossed the phone onto the passenger seat as the truck slammed into my car a third time. Metal screeched. *Think, Summer. You're intelligent. Get yourself out of this. 911!*

The truck slowed in preparation for another hit, and I swerved across the median into oncoming traffic, thanking God it wasn't rush hour. The white face of a woman driving a minivan sped past me. The driver tossed her hand up in an obscene gesture. Not what I needed at the moment.

The truck followed. I checked my rearview mirror, trying to see if a man or woman drove. A man, I thought. But I couldn't be sure. The person wore a baseball cap and a dark shirt.

Grabbing my cell phone, I struggled to concentrate on driving and dialing 911. My fingers pressed the numbers, and another slam whipped my head. The phone dropped into the seat. I stomped on the brakes so the car wouldn't be thrown into a spin. Tires squealed, and the air filled with the smell of burning rubber. A sob rose in my throat and stuck.

Horns blared as cars sped past us. My gaze swept the freeway ahead of me. Where were the police when you needed them? I swerved to miss an approaching car and steered back to the right side of the median.

"Please, God." A tinny jingle of "Onward, Christian Soldiers" rang out, and I grabbed for my phone.

"Ethan. Thank the Lord." I propped the phone between my cheek and shoulder and grasped the wheel with both hands.

"You called?"

"I'm on the freeway between Oak Hollow and Mountain Shadows. There's a truck that keeps rear-ending me." Tears streamed down my face, and I rubbed my cheek against my shoulder.

"Stay on the freeway. Don't let the truck force you off the road or onto a side road. Do you understand?"

"Yes. Ow! They're really hitting me hard, Ethan. I'm having a tough time controlling the wheel." Tires screamed as the truck pulled alongside me, trying to force me over. "This plastic thing I drive isn't going to hold much longer. Ethan!" My tires smoked.

"Did you call the police?"

"Almost. You're the first person I thought of." *You're always the first.* My knuckles hurt from the strain of gripping the wheel.

"Okay. Hang on, Summer. I'm going to dial Joe from the house phone."

"Don't leave me, Ethan."

"I won't. I promise."

Ethan shouted my name before my car veered out of control and smashed into a tree.

14

The strong odor of antiseptic assailed my nostrils, and I opened my eyes to dim lighting. My head ached, and I groaned, feeling nauseated. Moving as little as possible, I looked around the room.

Curtains in stripes of mint green and salmon surrounded my bed, cutting off my portion of the room. They'd clamped my index finger with one of those gadgets used for checking oxygen levels. A monitor beeped softly.

I groaned again and reached for the remote to raise the bed. My head swam, increasing the nausea. I scouted the nearby area for the little plastic tray they provide for that particular unpleasant business.

"Summer. Sweetie." Aunt Eunice popped up from a chair to my right. "What do you need? Can I get you anything?"

"What happened?" The bed whirred until I reached a reclined sitting position. "I'm sick to my stomach."

"What do you remember?" She handed me the salmon-colored plastic bowl.

I closed my eyes, remaining as still as possible until the nausea subsided.

Events played through my mind like a slide show. "A truck wouldn't stop slamming into me. I called Ethan. That's all I remember."

A large hand covered mine, and I opened my eyes to stare into Ethan's sapphire ones. Amazing how the sight of those blue eyes calmed me. Rooted me. "You were on the phone with me. Then nothing. Joe found your car wrapped around a tree on the side of the highway." He raised his free hand to smooth the hair from my forehead.

The tenderness in his eyes caused tears to well in my own. "Am I going to be all right?"

"You'll be colorfully painted around the eyes for a few days, and you've got a nasty goose egg on your forehead. Other than that, and the concussion, you'll be fine." A dimple winked in his right cheek. "I can't say the same for your car."

Tears beckoned. "I loved that car."

"Honey, the important thing is you're all right. The accident could've killed you. God's angels definitely surrounded you." Aunt Eunice fluffed my pillows. "I'll call the nurse to let the doctor know you're awake. He said you can probably go home in the morning."

I nodded. Aunt Eunice waddled out of the room, and I blinked away the tears. My head hurt, and I'd welcome something for the pain.

Ethan bent forward and laid a soft kiss on my cheek. "I've told your aunt I'll pick you up tomorrow. That way she can head in and open the store."

I nodded. "Thank you."

He caressed my cheek and was gone. I felt bereft and abandoned.

I woke the next morning to birds twittering outside the window and a cotton feeling in my mouth. I was alone. I didn't remember the nurse returning with medication, just nameless faces peering at me through the night. My aching head told me it was possible she hadn't. The doctor popped in, we'd spoken, and he released me. That, I remembered.

Outside my room nurses talked in groups, coffee mugs in hand. A phone rang. A beeper went off.

The prior day's events unfolded. I was certain I'd never seen the black truck before and not being interested in vehicles, I couldn't tell anyone what make or model it was. Who wanted me injured, or worse? Sure, someone had made things difficult for me lately, but to want me dead? What had I done?

The words of the mattress salesman came back to me. Mabel had said I didn't have much time. Were those her words or his interpretation of them? I shook my head, fighting back the nausea the movement caused. I needed to speak with Mabel.

They had unhooked me from the IV and other equipment. A fresh set of clothes lay folded on the nightstand. I slid my legs over the side of the bed and shrugged out of the hospital gown and into my clothes.

Short of breath, I lay back on the bed. Who would have thought a knock on the head could make a person so tired? I closed my eyes, intending to rest for a moment.

"Summer." Joe stood at the foot of my bed. "Are you up to answering some questions?"

My eyes popped open. "Hello, Joe. Yes, I'm fine. So kind of you to ask."

"Sorry." He sat in the chair beside my bed. "You look terrible."

I put a hand to my head, feeling the unruly mess. "Yeah, someone told me I've got a couple of black eyes."

"That's not all. There's a pretty nasty gash on your forehead. Took stitches."

Stitches? My hand flew to my forehead. Why hadn't I discovered the bandage before now? Would it leave a scar? Depression settled in as quickly as the arrival of Christmas. "What do you want to know, Joe?"

He pulled a small spiral notepad from his pocket. "What did the automobile that struck you look like? Did you catch the make and model? The license plate number?"

"Slow down. You're making me dizzy. It was a big black thing. Maybe an SUV. The truck was behind me. I didn't catch the license plate."

"Did you get a glimpse of the driver? Male or female?"

I ran both hands through the matted mess on my head. "I couldn't tell. My car sits low; the truck was high. I caught one glimpse of someone wearing a baseball cap. I called Ethan. That's all I remember." The questions made my head throb. "You need to look closer at Mabel."

Joe looked up from his pad. "Why?"

"She told the manager at the mattress store I didn't have much time."

"Time for what?"

"I don't know. But it sounds kind of fishy, considering someone tried to kill me."

"I shouldn't tell you this, Summer, but"—Joe closed the room door—"Ruby claims someone stole her SUV."

"Claims?"

"Well, I thought it unusual she waited two days to report the vehicle stolen. Two hours after you were admitted to the hospital."

I gnawed the inside of my lower lip. Was it possible

one of those old ladies was the diamond thief? That one of them broke into my house and outran me? Possible. I did trip over the dog. And the person did stop to hide their coveralls and gloves in the shed. Maybe they feared getting caught and didn't want to take the chance of leaving my property wearing the coveralls and gloves.

"Has anyone found Terri Lee?"

Joe shook his head. "Her mother's worried. Terri Lee isn't just hanging out with someone. She always calls home."

"Maybe she's behind all this. We haven't found her body. Dead or alive."

"Well, anything's possible." Joe snapped his notebook closed. "Ethan's pulling the car around front to take you home. He'll be here in a minute."

He stuffed the notebook into his pocket and fidgeted from foot to foot. "You're onto something, Summer, and someone's running scared. Please let me put you, Uncle Roy, and Aunt Eunice into protective custody."

A warm flush washed over me. "Why, Joe, you do care. I may not be the expert here, but I don't think you'll catch anyone if I'm hidden away somewhere."

"I hate to admit it, but you may be the bait to crack this case. We need you alive and kicking. Ethan has graciously offered to undertake the job of being your bodyguard." He tossed me a smile and left the room, holding the door open for Ethan.

Great. Now I'm bait. I'd definitely be discussing this with Joe once I was on my feet. Only the thought of my handsome, sent-from-heaven bodyguard could dispel my irritation.

"Are you ready?" Ethan planted a gentle kiss on my

forehead, dodging the bandage. Last night, the cheek. Today, the forehead. I was tempted never to wash my face again.

"More than ready." I accepted the hand he offered and allowed him to help me to my feet. My legs wobbled, and Ethan placed an arm around my waist. If I'd known how good this would feel, I'd have been hospitalized a long time ago.

"There's a wheelchair right outside the door." Ethan steered me out of the room and helped me get situated in the vinyl and steel contraption.

It was embarrassing to imagine people staring when Ethan rolled me from the hospital and into his waiting pickup. I'm sure I could've walked, given the chance.

"Home?" Ethan asked as he helped me into the vehicle.

"No. Take me by Mabel's. I've got some questions to ask her."

Ethan slid into the driver's seat. "Summer." He turned the key in the ignition.

I crossed my arms. "As my bodyguard, you have to take me where I want. You know I'll go without you the first chance I get."

He sighed and put the truck into gear. "What's so important that it has to be done today?"

I clicked my seat belt and turned my head to glance at him. "Did Joe tell you what she said? That I didn't have much time left? At least that's what the mattress guy said she said."

"You know how things get distorted."

"That's why I want to ask her directly."

"Fine. But the doctor said you're supposed to be

resting." He steered the truck from the parking lot to the highway. "One way or the other, you're going to drag me into this, aren't you?"

"Can I?"

Believe it or not, Ethan rolled his eyes. I thought only women did that. "I'm here, aren't I? All right. Tell me what you know."

Excitement overcame me. My face hurt from the grin I wore. "Aunt Eunice told me—well, screamed it actually—that I should ask God who to put on my suspect list. Here are the people and why. Terri Lee, because she's missing, she works with diamonds, and she's just plain mean."

Ethan cleared his throat, and I'm pretty certain his lips twitched.

"Also, Richard Bland. I've never met him, but he's a diamond broker, also missing, and the police have found his car. Mabel Coffman has a Cadillac. There's no way she could pay for that car on her pension and part-time salary. Same for Ruby Colville's diamond ring."

"What about Nate?"

"Nate? Why should he be on the suspect list?"

Ethan tossed me a glance before refocusing on his driving. "Because he's new to town. We don't know anything about him. Just because he's courting you—"

I shook my head. "Your imagination is really something. Nate isn't—"

"*My* imagination? Joe has probably checked out all these suspects of yours."

"He's missing something. Told me so himself."

"And if the police can't find out who the culprit is, what makes you think you can?"

"Because 'the culprit' isn't after the police. He's after me."

Ethan started to say something but clamped his mouth closed as we pulled into Mabel's driveway. No Cadillac sat parked in front of the gray wood-shingled house. Pink impatiens overflowed wooden barrels. She had swept the porch clean. I stuck my head out the open window of the truck and listened. Nothing. "She's not here."

"It does appear that way. Can I take you home now?"

"We could go by the paper."

"No. If you still want to, we can go tomorrow. Today I'm taking you home to bed."

My cheeks heated at his innocent words, and I sent a quick prayer heavenward for forgiveness at the direction my thoughts had traveled. But to be honest, Ethan should be gracing the cover of *People* magazine's "Sexiest Man Alive" issue.

The object of my thoughts backed the truck from the drive. "What's on your mind?"

My face stung with heat. He caught me. "Nothing. Just thinking about everything."

He chuckled.

"What?"

"Nothing." He snorted with the effort to hold back his laughter.

Had he guessed what I'd been thinking? I turned to stare out the window. How could I ever look at him again? Did he know what he'd said? Was it not an accident? Had the man no sense of embarrassment? He was a volunteer at church! I straightened in my seat. Was he flirting with me? The car grew warm. I cracked my window.

The sight of Aunt Eunice pacing the front porch of our house pulled me from my musings. The sweet woman had closed the store early to welcome me home. "Thank the Lord!" She jogged toward us, her face red with the effort. She waved a white piece of paper in her hand. "This is for you, Summer. I found it on the porch when I woke up this morning."

As I read the note, my heart skipped a beat. Someone had cut words out of a magazine and pasted them on notebook paper. I read them out loud. *"Bring the cash to the highway underpass at 11:00 p.m. on Saturday. Come alone or suffer the consequences."*

I glanced at Ethan. "This is Saturday. I don't have the cash. Joe took it and gave it to that other cop." I narrowed my eyes at him. "I told you we should've kept it. Now what?"

"Stop talking, give prayer a try, and let me think. Lord, give me patience." Ethan lowered himself to the top porch step, the note in his hand. "Call Joe. Get him over here."

Aunt Eunice rushed into the house to do his bidding, returning seconds later with the cordless phone in her hand. "He'll be right here. I'll whip up something to eat."

"Food. Her solution to everything. Or tea. She uses that a lot, too." I joined Ethan on the top step. My head ached, and I leaned to rest on his shoulder. He placed his arm around me, pulling me close.

"Don't worry, Tink. I won't let anyone hurt you. I'll be right beside you."

"As wonderful as that sounds, Ethan, it's impossible. The note said for me to come alone."

"No chance." His arm tightened.

"What if something bad happens?"

"We'll get through it together."

I loved the sound of that. We sat in silence until Joe's car rolled into the driveway. Ethan got to his feet, keeping his hand on my shoulder.

"What did Summer do now?" Joe scowled.

"I'm right here. You don't have to talk over me, and I didn't do anything. We got this." I snatched the paper from Ethan's hand and gave it to Joe.

If Joe was the kind of man who swore, I'm sure choice words would've come from his mouth. The man needed a vacation. Especially after this week. His face had turned scarlet on so many occasions lately, I feared for his health.

"Well? What am I supposed to do?" I stepped away from Ethan and stared into my cousin's worry-lined face.

Joe rubbed a hand over the stubble of his hair. "I'm a small-town cop. I didn't sign up for this. It's time to call in the big guys. I'm suggesting Wayne call the state police."

"I didn't sign up for this either. Someone is trying to kill me, Joe."

He glared at me. "I realize that. My main concern is to keep you safe."

"Give me the money back. I'll turn it over tonight."

"I can't. It's locked up."

I gnawed my lip. "I got it. I'll scan a twenty-dollar bill, make copies, and try to fool the crooks that way." Ethan and Joe looked at me as if I'd lost my mind.

"You're playing with the law." Joe shook his head. "That's counterfeiting."

"I'm not going to spend the money." Now my head pounded. I sat back on the stoop. "You come up with something better."

Joe glanced at his watch. "That's six hours from now. Plenty of time to find out what the state police want us to do. Let me go back to the station, call them, and head out here when I'm off duty. The other officers at the station can handle the little things. Okay?"

"Can't you call them now? On your cell phone?"

"I'd rather have privacy."

"Fine." At this point, I didn't care. I wanted the bed Ethan promised me. He must have taken notice of my exhaustion. He pulled me to my feet.

"Summer has a busy night ahead. She's got to get some rest." He steered me into the house and shouted for Aunt Eunice to help me. "I'll be here when you wake up," he promised, laying a soft kiss on my cheek.

I nodded and allowed my aunt to lead me up the stairs and tuck me into bed like a small child. This was becoming commonplace. Like I was reverting in age, rather than moving forward.

The manager, bless his heart, had rush-delivered my mattress, and I sank into it like a baby in a bassinet. A new down pillow, a free gift with the purchase, cradled my head. Within seconds, to soft murmurs of Aunt Eunice praying, I drifted into slumberland.

A knock on the door caused my eyes to fly open. I glanced at the clock. *10:00*. My aunt poked her head in. "The police are here and ready for you. You might want to take one of your pain pills. They're a stiff bunch."

15

Two men and a woman, all wearing dark suits, clustered in the living room. Another man in black slacks and a white long-sleeved shirt sat in front of a laptop. I scanned the room to locate Ethan. He and Joe stood by the front door, looking like misplaced children at an adult party.

"Miss Meadows?" The woman approached me, her dark hair drawn into a tight bun and her face devoid of makeup. Cocoa brown eyes stared impassively into mine. "We'd like for you to have a seat on the sofa." She motioned toward one of the men, the older of the two. "Mr. Brown will talk you through tonight's proceedings."

I covered my mouth to hide a snicker. For a police officer's name, Mr. Brown seemed a bit cliché, but who was I to argue? I must look terrible. Mister Stern Face relaxed before perching next to me. I raised a hand to my face. *Yep. Definitely puffy.* My head swam from the effects of the painkillers.

"Don't be frightened, Miss Meadows. We'll have you under surveillance the entire time. Officer Bowers," he motioned his head toward the woman, "will put a wire on you that will enable us to hear everything that goes on."

"I'm not afraid, Officer Brown." My lips curled into a smile. "Greater is He who is in me than he who is in the world." The expression on the man's face showed he didn't have a whole lot of faith, if any. "Okay, I'm a little nervous."

"As you should be. There has already been one

attempt on your life." Officer Brown stood. "You'll be carrying a bag of marked bills. If anyone approaches you, do exactly as they say. Don't be brave. Don't try taking them down."

Taking them down? Who did he think I was, a superhero?

The doorbell rang. Officer Brown placed a restraining hand on my shoulder. At his nod, Aunt Eunice stepped up and answered the door. She then turned and hid back in the kitchen.

Nate pushed himself inside, only to find his path blocked by every testosterone-packing male in the place. "I want to see Summer. I need to know she's all right."

I brushed Officer Brown's hand from my shoulder and stood. "I'm fine, Nate. Now isn't a good time."

"Are you in trouble? I want to be here with you."

"You heard the lady." Officer Wayne gave him a soft shove out the door and locked the dead bolt. "How did he get all the way to the porch? Where's outside security? Any more visitors going to show up at this time of the night?" He sneered. "Way to keep things undercover."

I shook my head. "He's my, er, former boyfriend." *Undercover?* I glanced out the window. The driveway housed both my aunt and uncle's truck, Ethan's pickup, and two dark-colored sedans. Definitely not undercover. It looked like a funeral wake out there. I wasn't crazy about the analogy.

With still nearly an hour to go before my appointment, I grew bored watching the silent agents doing whatever they did. With all eyes on me, I ambled toward Joe and Ethan. "Any news no one's told me yet?"

There had to be. The two had been whispering since

I came downstairs. "Well?"

Ethan leaned forward to whisper in my ear. His breath tickled the hair on my neck. "The fingerprint on the wooden box from your tree house was Terri Lee's."

"Ethan!" Joe crossed his arms. "That's the last time I tell you anything."

"I'd have dragged the information from you sooner or later. You never could keep a secret. How you became a police officer, I'll never know." I peeked over my shoulder at the police wraiths floating around the room. "I knew she was guilty. Now we just have to find her."

An almost-overwhelming sense of gratification washed over me. If my grin got any bigger, my face would have split in two. I wasn't doing too badly at this investigating business. If Terri Lee showed up to collect the money tonight, they'd close the case, and I could refocus on the candy store.

"Miss Meadows?" Officer Bowers approached me with some wire contraption in her hands. "We're ready to get you wired."

"A venti mocha latte will do that." I giggled, thinking myself clever. Apparently, the medication still made me loopy. I was the only one laughing.

I held my arms straight out from my sides. "Let's do this."

The woman's face paled, and she glanced at the group of men. "It would be better if we did this in another room. You'll have to remove your shirt."

Idiot. "Of course." My face heated. "Don't you police officers have a sense of humor?"

"Not while we're working, Miss Meadows." Officer Bowers waved her hand for me to precede her. "You need to wear a baggy blouse. It'll hide the wire more effectively."

"We can also stuff it in my cleavage, if you know what I mean. God hasn't exactly deprived me in that area." I snorted at my cleverness and delusion of grandeur.

"Are you sure you're up to this, Miss Meadows? Are you on medication?"

"Painkillers. Aren't they great? I really don't care about anything." I opened the door to the bathroom and grabbed a navy blouse from where I'd draped it over the clothes hamper the day before. "This one will work. It's big, baggy, and buttons up the front."

Ms. Police Officer rolled her eyes at me as she shut the door. "Strip down to your bra. Let me get this hooked on you."

"But I hardly know you." I snickered then quit at the stony silence greeting my joke. Really, I'd have to discuss the police's lack of humor with Mr. Brown.

Brown stepped up to us as soon as we reentered the living room. "Don't forget, Miss Meadows. We'll have you in our sights the entire time. If someone approaches you and you fear for your life, turn and run. We'll be there in seconds. Under no circumstances should you leave the area with anyone but one of my officers. Understand?"

"Perfectly, sir!" I saluted and sobered when I caught the frightened look on Ethan's face. His skin turned the color of creamed wheat beneath his tan. The silly man did care for me. The thought warmed me, overpowering the niggling fear quickly rising. What was I doing? The medication had nothing to do with my goofiness. I was terrified and trying desperately to cover up the fact.

"Showtime, folks." Brown clapped his hands and,

before I knew it, ushered me outside and into a van that appeared on the property as if by magic.

I glanced toward the house. Ethan stood outlined in the light of the front door. Joe clapped him on the shoulder, and the two sprinted to Joe's squad car. I felt safer knowing Ethan would be close by. Silly, considering the others were trained professionals. But knowing there would be at least two people near the underpass who really cared about me, not because it was part of their job, left me more secure.

Aunt Eunice waved from the kitchen window. She lifted her apron and dabbed at her eyes. Trying to solve this case on my own affected my family, as well.

Lord, forgive me for my selfishness. Keep my family and me safe from my stupidity.

"Wouldn't it make more sense for me to drive myself? I mean, if the suspect sees me getting out of a van and knows I drive a Sonata, and my aunt and uncle own trucks—"

"Miss Meadows, we have it all worked out so they don't know what you'll be driving. You'll be fine. Besides, the last time you drove, someone ran you off the road. It'll be dark. We'll drop you off approximately fifty feet from where you need to be. You can walk the rest of the way. We'll be watching you every minute."

Brown gave me a wink. I think he meant to reassure me. It left me gaping like a fish, since the man's face screwed up like a dried tomato. He obviously couldn't wink. Then he slammed the rear door, casting me into darkness.

Within seconds, a dim light burned over my head, and I released the breath I held. *God, be with me. God, be with me.*

We arrived a few minutes later. The van door swung open. Brown held a finger to his lips and helped me disembark. With my feet firmly planted on the asphalt, I looked for Joe's squad car. No sign of it. My stomach plummeted.

Humidity hung like a heavy blanket in the Southern summer night, and I shivered from the van's air-conditioning. Only the stars lit the two-lane highway. Brother moon was hiding. A bullfrog croaked from a nearby pond. Simple sounds that would comfort on a normal night.

I walked toward the underpass, my tennis shoes pounding dully against the road. I moved closer to my destination, the rapid beat of my heart drowning out the noises of unseen creatures.

Not a car in sight. I had no idea where to stand. On the side of the road? In the middle?

The painkillers were wearing off, along with my flippant attitude. Fear crept in and took up residence in the center of my chest. The night grew silent. I lost track of how long I waited before loneliness set in. And I mean a deep loneliness. The kind that makes you think you're the last living thing on the planet.

All cooling from the air conditioner was gone by now, and I lifted a hand to wipe my forehead. Maybe if I talked to myself, it would relieve my boredom and fear. "I need a sidekick. Miss Marple had. . . I don't know whether she had one or not. Maybe that detective guy. Nancy Drew had Bess and George. Sherlock had Holmes. No, that's his last name. Watson. Sherlock had Watson."

I paced up and down the middle of the road until my feet ached. "I definitely need a sidekick. Well, I suppose one would say God was my sidekick, but I'm not sure that's appropriate. I'd rather He sat in the driver's seat, and I could be the passenger."

But then I'd have to take my hands off the steering wheel. Was I ready? Could I give God total control?

Headlights broke the black, and I scurried to the side of the road. A low-slung car of howling teenage boys roared past. I took deep breaths to steady my heartbeat.

I held my breath as they turned around. I tilted my head to speak into the microphone. "Huh, guys, there's a car full of teenagers heading for me. They're slowing down. They're stopping."

"Hey, lady!" One young man, a liter bottle of something that didn't resemble soda, leaned out the window. "You all right? You been in a car accident or something?"

"No, I'm fine, thank you."

"Are you sure? You look like you've been beat up, and your neck is crooked. Do you need a ride somewhere?"

I straightened, glad the shadows hid my flaming face. "No, I'm meeting someone."

"Oh." His eyes widened. "I get it. She's having a secret rendezvous."

The guys in the car roared with laughter, and I grinned. "You guessed it. Bye now."

The taillights disappeared down the road. I pushed the button on my watch to illuminate the face. *11:14.* Had I only been out here a half hour?

I lowered into a seated position and wrapped my arms around my knees. Maybe this was a wild-goose chase. What if they'd planned to lure me away from home? What if I wasn't the intended target? They could be after Uncle Roy or Aunt Eunice. I bolted to my feet and paced. The thought terrified me.

"Hey, officers." I dipped my chin to speak into my chest. My voice bounced off the concrete overpass. "What if I'm not the target?" No answer. I guessed it to be a one-way wire. What was the range on these? *Horror.* Had they heard me talking to myself?

Of course they had. If the crook did show up, he or she wouldn't be speaking into my chest. The wire would have to pick up the sound from at least a couple of feet. *Thank You, Lord, that I didn't speak about my feelings for Ethan aloud.* It was embarrassing enough that he heard everything else I'd rattled on about.

A vehicle loomed on the horizon. Its headlights sliced through the darkness. The car paused at the top of the hill, engine roaring through the night. I shielded my eyes and stepped into the center of the road.

"This is it, guys." I didn't dip my chin this time.

The noise grew in intensity. The car, maybe a Cadillac, lurched forward and, picking up speed, raced in my direction.

"He's trying to hit me—to run me over! Get out here and stop him!" I scurried up the embankment, scraping the palms of my hands. Finally, at the top, breathing heavy from exertion and fear, I scooped up a fist-sized rock, wound up like a major leaguer, and hurled it.

Strike! The rock bounced off the cracked windshield. My smile was a mile long at the satisfying crunch sound. "You want me? Come and get me, coward!"

I bent to retrieve another rock but looked up at the sound of a car door opening.

"Y'all, he's getting out. I have to admit I'm scared

and in no shape to outrun someone."

No response.

"Can you see this? You said you'd keep me in your sights."

Please let me be in their sights. My heart sprang to my throat, choking my words.

"He's opening the back door and pulling on something. . . . Wait, he's dragging something out. Something heavy."

I straightened. "He's waving at me."

Confusion clouded my mind. My hand rose to return the gesture; then I clenched my fist beside me. Did that mean he knew me? I stopped my monologue. The shadowy, dark figure hopped back in the car. "He's leaving."

I stared at the lump he'd deposited. It looked like one of those black lawn and leaf bags at first. When I got closer, I realized I'd mistaken a blanket-wrapped bundle for a bag. "Should I go check it out?" I'd already begun my sliding descent down the hill. The agents couldn't answer anyway. Why wait for them?

Only one way to find out what it was. I squatted in front of the bundle. "I'm opening it now."

In my head, in my imagination, I could hear the officers screaming at me not to touch it. I couldn't resist and reached for the fabric, pulling it aside.

I screamed. The sound reverberated.

Terri Lee stared at me with the black, lifeless sheen of a doll's eyes.

16

I stumbled back, landing on my bottom. Even in the light from the stars, I could see the gash across Terri Lee's neck. The pavement beneath her shone from the blood spilling from the blanket. My hand was wet from where I'd gripped it. I wiped it on my jeans.

"Summer!" Ethan ran up and slid to the ground beside me. "Are you all right? Are you hurt?" He grabbed me and pulled me to him.

Pointing at the bundle, I gulped the night air. "It's Terri Lee." I peered up at him. "She's stuffed in there." I pointed again. "Like somebody's discarded trash."

Within seconds, police swarmed the area, flashlights waving. Officer Bowers draped a blanket around me. It smelled of cigarettes and coffee. I stared at my shoes, spattered crimson. The same red seeped into the bottom edge of the blanket. I shuddered, stomach churning.

Ethan ran his hands up and down my arms briskly. I wasn't cold, but it felt so nice. "You're so strong, Summer."

I shook my head, trying not to watch Terri Lee's body being placed in a bag. "I'm not. Not really." Tears ran down my cheeks, soaking his shirt. "I'm afraid, Ethan. I acted brave, but that wasn't me. That was the painkillers. They aren't working anymore. My hand hurts. My head hurts, and I'm scared out of my mind." I raised my voice with each word.

He pulled me close. "Shh. I'm here. I'll take care of you."

My gaze fell on the zipped body bag holding Terri Lee's remains lit by the headlights of the van the officers had pulled up. "I don't want to end up like her."

"You won't. I promise." His grip tightened to where my nose pressed against him. He smelled of cologne and sweat.

"Ethan, I can't breathe."

"Sorry." He loosened his hold. I turned my head. He held me close. His heart beat in time with my breathing. I didn't want to leave the security of his arms.

"Miss Meadows, we have a couple of questions." Officer Brown squatted next to us.

I didn't want to speak to him. Ethan kept the blanket wrapped around me as I pulled back. "Didn't y'all hear everything through the wire?"

"Yes, but we couldn't see. You were our eyes."

The image of Terri Lee's face swam before me. I wondered whether I'd remember anything else. Unfortunately, the details came flooding back, and I told Officer Brown everything. His pen scratched across the paper pad he held. "Are you sure you saw a man?"

I wrapped my arms around my knees. I suppose a woman could've pulled the body from the car. But he, or she, looked bigger than any woman I know. I shrugged. "Pretty sure."

"We need more than 'pretty sure,' Miss Meadows." Officer Brown had the audacity to frown at me. After all I'd done for him.

Ethan bolted to his feet. "That's enough, Brown. Summer's going home. Any questions you have can wait until tomorrow. Officer Wayne can come question her then." He held out a hand to help me up. With his arm around my shoulders, Ethan led me to Joe's squad car.

Exhaustion washed over me, filling my limbs with lead. Once Ethan scooted beside me in the backseat, I snuggled under his arm and laid my head on his chest. Before my eyes closed, I'd swear I heard him say he'd be my sidekick.

My eyes opened to the view of my bedroom ceiling. The last thing I remembered was Ethan carrying me upstairs. Then Aunt Eunice getting me ready for bed.

I swung my legs over the side of the bed and groaned. Every inch of my body hurt. The cut on my hand, the scrapes on my knees, every muscle from my head-on with the tree.

The *Dolt* book caught my eye. *Ugh!* I swiped it from the nightstand to the floor. It hadn't helped so far. Maybe I wasn't being entirely fair. The couple of ideas I'd followed had unveiled information. Today, with all my aches, investigating didn't take top priority.

Being Sunday, I opted for church and then a relaxing afternoon in bed. What could I wear to cover my battle scars? My glance fell on a long summer dress. One that brushed my ankles. I couldn't do better. Plus, it looked pretty. Pink with little blue sprigs of flowers.

I spent fifteen minutes trying to style my hair to hide the black-and-blue marks. My bangs fell forward, obscuring my vision. I needed a haircut. With a sigh, I pinned them up out of my face, leaving bangs to hide my stitches. It wouldn't do for me to fall and add to my injuries. It would be just my luck to fall and break a leg. Maybe both.

Uncle Roy appeared at the bottom of the stairs. "Wait right there. I don't want you climbing down by yourself." He hurried up, his booted feet clunking on the wood.

Grasping me by the elbow, he led me down one step at a time.

A sweet gesture, really. Made me feel cherished. Loved.

"Thank you, Uncle Roy."

"How you feeling, darling?"

"Sore. Tired. But I'll be all right." At the bottom, I cupped a hand over his cheek. "I love you, Uncle Roy. I appreciate you. Have I told you?"

His work-worn hand covered mine. "Honey, there's no need. I know you do." Tears welled in his eyes. "I love you, too."

"I'm going to cry." Aunt Eunice stood in the doorway of the kitchen, her hands clasped over her heart.

I smiled and hugged her. "I love you, Aunt Eunice."

The hug she returned threatened to crack my ribs. "Oh, sweetie." She released me and stepped back. "Let's go eat breakfast and get to church. We could all use a big ole dose of worship."

⌘

The ride to church wrapped me in the warmth of love. The love of God and my family. Tears hovered behind my eyelids the entire time.

Ethan met us in the parking lot and helped me from the truck. The tender look on his face had my hidden tears escaping in no time. I wiped them away. I'd been wrong about the big doofus for years. He loved me. But why didn't he say anything to me?

My caring protector got me settled comfortably in a pew beside my aunt before heading back to the atrium to resume his duties. Confusion clouded my mind. Days before, all the solicitous attention would've offended me. Made me uncomfortable. Embarrassed. Not anymore.

What changed me? I wanted to say maturity, but that couldn't be the reason. I would be thirty soon. How much more mature could I get? And poor Terri Lee. I was even more convinced she was guilty, but no one deserved to be murdered and dumped on the side of the road.

I remained seated during worship, my mind going over the events of last night. Had I given the police all the vital information? Why had the suspect wanted me to deliver the money if he didn't intend to collect it? Had he come to leave Terri Lee's body as a message for me? For the police?

I tuned in to the pastor's words. I'd missed most of what he'd said, being lost in my musings, but the part about not leaning on one's own understanding riveted me.

It hit me like a knock over the head. That's what I'd been doing. Had I asked God to help me with this case? Nope. Doubly important now that someone obviously wanted me out of the picture.

I choked back a laugh remembering Aunt Eunice's orders to ask God who should be on my list of suspects. She'd be livid to discover Ruby and Mabel topped said list. Especially with Terri Lee among the deceased.

I turned to greet Ethan with a smile as he sat next to me partway through the message. He leaned closer to whisper, "How are you holding up?"

"Fine. Just listening." He had never joined me for

a service before. It felt natural. "I've realized I need to have a conversation with God about this case. It's long overdue."

Ethan's face set into what resembled a handsome marble cast of his head. "I wish you'd stop trying to solve this."

"I can't. Somebody wants me dead." The thought chilled me to the core. "They won't stop even if I do."

He wrapped my hand in his. "I know. But I don't like it."

"Besides"—I gave his hand a squeeze—"I have a trusty bodyguard now." I excused myself before the service ended, wanting to beat the after-service restroom rush.

No one else was in the bathroom. Trembling overtook me. I chose the farthest stall from the door and perched on the closed lid of the toilet. Now seemed a good a time as any to have a conversation with the Lord. I prayed no one would interrupt my stolen quiet time.

Tears coursed a path down my cheeks. Knowing someone hated me enough to want me dead baffled me. I'd grown up having people love me. I needed help. With everything. A spark of anger burned toward April. She'd promised to be my partner in this. Instead, she'd become all google-eyed over Joe. Again, my fault.

Remorse flooded over me. How could I wish the danger threatening me on someone else?

Lord, I can't do this alone anymore. I never should've started without calling on You. I'm scared. I'm experiencing emotions completely alien to me. I need Your help. Protect me, please. Ethan has affection for me. I want to live long enough to enjoy it.

The door scraped as it opened. I grabbed a handful

of tissues and wiped my tears, remaining still, silent. I hoped no one would know I occupied the stall. I couldn't carry a coherent conversation.

Whoever had hit against the door apparently decided against entry. A final grate and the room was quiet again. I'd spent enough time in here. Ethan would wonder and worry.

I pushed open the stall door and stepped to the sink. Someone believed in pampering the ladies of the church, and I squirted some rose-scented soap into my hands. I glanced in the mirror and cringed. Red, swollen eyes stared back at me. I'd totally ruined my makeup. I thanked God I was at church. Swollen eyes and streaked faces were common after a moving sermon or worship.

After drying my hands with a wad of paper towels, I pushed against the door. It didn't budge. I shoved harder but couldn't move the heavy panel of wood. Stepping back, I chewed my lower lip. Had someone locked me in? I glanced at my watch. Ten more minutes and someone would discover the locked door. Women would be swarming in here.

I lowered my aching, scratched, and weary body into one of the padded chairs provided for nursing mothers. How long until Ethan worried? I dug into my purse for my orange-flavored mints. Anything to keep my mind off being locked in the restroom. And at church. Was nothing sacred?

Footsteps approached. My heart quickened; then my shoulders slumped as the steps retreated. The place should be crowded by now. I stood and tried the door again. *Nothing. Lord, I really need someone to miss me about now.*

I doubled my fist and pounded. "Hello? Anybody?"

Voices sounded from the other side. Why couldn't they hear me? "Hey!" I knocked harder, stopping when my fist hurt. I gave a kick before resuming my seat.

A screech and the door opened. I bolted to my feet, relieved to see Aunt Eunice standing there, her eyes wide.

"Someone locked me in!"

"I see that, dear." She stepped aside and showed where a metal sign was propped beneath the door handle. A hanging piece of paper read OUT OF ORDER.

Behind my aunt, the members of the church stood staring at me. Well, maybe not all three thousand of them, but the people on my suspect list were there. I glared at everyone until Ethan pushed his way through and took me by the elbow to the courtyard.

"Where were you?"

"I needed to take care of something. I thought you'd be safe in the restroom."

I planted my fists on my hips. "Well, I wasn't."

"You were only locked in the ladies' room. Could have been worse." He escorted me to the parking lot and steered me toward the car.

"Why?"

"Why what?"

"Why would someone lock me in the restroom? At church?" I tugged against his hold on me. "It doesn't make sense. Stop."

He turned to face me.

"I think a member of this church murdered Terri Lee. Joe needs to question everyone."

"All of them? Summer, you aren't being realistic. Besides, the police are investigating. They know what to do. And how do you know it's someone from church?"

Ethan patted his pockets, sighed, and released me. "I left my cell phone in the church office. Sit here on the bench. I've got a couple of phone calls to make. Do you have your cell?" I shook my head. "You ought to be safe enough here in plain sight."

He bent and stared at me. "Don't move. I mean it. I'll send your aunt or my sister over. Whoever I find first." He brushed my hair back from my face. "Please, don't move from this spot."

Neither came soon enough. Duane Parker stared at me from across the courtyard. I smiled a welcome, remembering Ethan's comment on convicting the man because of his past. Duane's lips disappeared into a thin line under his beard. I shivered at the cold look in his eyes before he turned his face away. Could the guy really still be carrying a grudge after all these years?

Several minutes later, Nate approached at a hurried pace, which led me to believe something concerned him. His attitude annoyed me. His brow furrowed into worry lines as he sat down, taking my hands in his.

"I heard about your car accident, Summer. Are you all right?"

"I'm fine. Just a little sore." I tried pulling away, but he held on with an iron grip.

"You've got to let me take care of you."

"No, that's—"

He raised a hand against my protests. "I insist, Summer. I know you're infatuated with Ethan, but that's all it is." His voice took on a sense of urgency. "He isn't caring for you properly. You need *me*."

Aunt Eunice exited the church, and I bolted to my

feet. "Aunt Eunice! Got to go, Nate." I called over my shoulder, "Thanks for being concerned."

I kissed my aunt's cheek. "Thank you. Thank you. Thank you." I glanced at Nate and shivered. A frigid look replaced the worry lines on his face.

"Where's Ethan?"

"Praying with someone in need. I'm going to take you home. Ready?"

"Ready and willing." I slung my arm around her waist. I froze a few steps from my aunt's truck.

In the parking space next to us sat a large-model car with a busted windshield. Was it the one I had shattered? I reached for my cell phone to call Joe. After all, he was family—even if he *was* off the case.

17

I gazed across the kitchen table at April. A breeze ruffled her curls from the open kitchen window. Duane's nightly ritual of walking down the highway whistling drifted to my ears. Concern marred her usually smooth features. Guilt clenched my heart. "I'm sorry."

"For what?" Her light brown brows drew together.

"I've been selfish." I gripped the frozen mocha drink she handed me. "I didn't think of the consequences before plunging headfirst into this case. God convicted me while I sat in the bathroom. Philippians 2:4 came to mind. 'Each of you should look not only to your own interests, but also to the interests of others.' " I took a gulp of the icy drink hoping to drown my sorrows. "I hadn't thought of how my actions would affect others. Aunt Eunice and Uncle Roy are worried sick. Ethan has to babysit—"

"Which you don't mind in the least." Azure eyes twinkled at me.

"Not really." I returned her smile. "Nevertheless, I should've thought of the consequences before. It was very irresponsible of me."

"Yep, and I haven't been much help. We have to catch this guy. What have you got?" She folded her hands on the table.

I slid my suspect list toward her. "Aunt Eunice got mad when I showed this to her."

"It isn't complete."

"What do you mean?"

"Where's mine and Ethan's name? Or your aunt? Uncle Roy?"

"You two aren't thieves or killers. Aunt Eunice can't stomp on a spider, and Uncle Roy—" My mind raced. He *had* been gone during a lot of my scares. No, there was no way the murderer could be my sweet uncle.

"I'll give you Ethan. He was with you when a couple of the incidents occurred, but I wasn't. I could easily be the thief." April handed the paper back to me.

"It's a man. I'm certain. A man definitely dumped Terri Lee's body on the side of the road." I folded the list and tucked it into my pocket.

"He could be my accomplice." April sat back in her chair. "The thing is, Summer, it could be anyone. Don't limit your suspects to those few names."

I twirled a straw in the soupy remains of whipped cream and coffee. My gut told me I was right about the suspect being male. My mind snapped back to the intruder in the house, who looked more like a woman in size and bone structure. There were two. Did Terri Lee's death put it back to one? "Sounds like Joe's teaching you about investigative work."

"Nah. I'm good at eavesdropping. He won't tell me a thing." April folded her arms across her chest. "He's frustrated about the dead ends the department keeps running up against. And he's champing at the bit because he's not in full control."

"They don't have any leads?" The thought floored me. If Joe didn't have a clue, how was I supposed to know anything?

April stood. "It'll work out. You'll be fine, I'll be fine, and everyone will be fine."

Terri Lee isn't fine. Her dead boyfriend isn't fine. I might not be fine, either. I wish I had her confidence. It wasn't that I didn't have faith. I did. As much as the next guy. It hadn't been tested until now. I planted my palms on the table and pushed to my feet. "You're right. I'm having a moment of weakness."

The crack of a twig sounded. I spun toward the open kitchen window. April gasped.

"I'm going out there to check." I took a step toward the door then stopped, remembering the other times I'd heard noises. April was right. There was absolutely no way I was going outside.

April clutched my arm. "No. It's like those scary movies. The girl goes to find out what's making the noise and gets killed. Horribly killed, in a really bloody way."

"Don't be ridiculous. It's probably my aunt or uncle."

"They said they were staying for the evening service. You heard them." She pulled me through the doorway and into the hall. "How do you stand it? Every other night, something happens. What are you? A danger magnet?"

"That's what I've been trying to tell you. No one is safe around me." I grabbed the phone and held it to April. "Call the police. We put Joe's number on speed dial, number 2."

April snatched the phone from my hand and pressed the buttons. "What do we do?"

"Wait, hide, and pray." I checked the lock on the front door then took April by the elbow and pulled her farther away from the window.

"Your phone battery's almost dead. Why can't you remember to keep it charged? I charge mine every night."

I stared at her like she'd gone crazy. "You're lecturing me about my phone at a time like this?"

Footsteps pounded as someone ran across the porch.

April opened her mouth to scream, and I clamped a hand over her lips. "Shh." She trembled. When did I get so strong? Feelings of obstinacy and anger grew in the pit of my stomach, sending heat over my neck and face. If I'd been alone, I'd have gone outside to confront the person who delighted in trying to frighten me. Easy to say. My limbs shook.

I flicked off the hall lamp and pulled April down to the floor with me. "We'll be fine. They always go away. It's a game."

More footsteps stampeded across the porch, and Truly shot from the upstairs landing to the front door. Her stocky body bristled with indignation, and her bark was shrill and frantic. I clapped my hands over my ears. "Truly. Here."

"Do you smell smoke?" I crawled toward the front door. Wispy gray tendrils snaked under the wood. I pushed to my feet and sprinted toward the back of the house. The same telltale odor alerted me. Flames towered outside the back door.

April joined me, her face shining pale in the gloom of the kitchen. "I'm going to call Joe again."

I'd like to think the man would hurry because there had been another intruder. Sometimes living in the country had its drawbacks. The dog's barking grated on my nerves, April's clutch on my upper arm promised to leave bruises, and the increasing amount of smoke burned my lungs.

"Tell me again why you want to discover the identity of the diamond thief?" April whispered.

"At this point, only God knows." I led my friend back to the hall where I scanned for something to throw through the front window. A footstool. That would be easy for me to lift. I glanced at April. "Pray."

"If you break the window, you'll let them in."

"We take that chance or die of smoke inhalation." I slammed the stool against the glass, rejoicing in the satisfying crack. One look at the towering flames on the porch reassured me no one would be coming in that way. I craned my neck. The fire burned in a line across the front porch. It hadn't touched the house yet.

But we couldn't get out that way.

"Upstairs. We'll climb out. We'll stand on the sill and leap to the tree." I dropped the stool and grabbed April's hand, before yelling for Truly to follow us. "Grab my purse. My cell phone's in it." April snagged the bag. I dragged her up the stairs.

I glanced at my watch. "It takes a few minutes for Joe to get here even on a good day. It's only been five."

Inside my room, I slammed the door closed, dragged April to the window, and stared down in dismay. The tree stood too far back. I turned to glance at the bed.

"Oh no! There's no way I'm climbing out with a rope of sheets tied around my waist. I'll break my neck. I'm not a good climber. I'm taking my chances waiting for Joe."

"You climbed to the tree house plenty of times."

"This is different. The tree house had steps, and I'm scared now. Look." She held her hand in front of her. "I'm shaking."

Sirens wailed in the distance, and Ethan appeared

below us. He cupped his hands around his mouth. "Wait there. I'll get the ladder."

Where did he think we'd go? Tears of relief welled in my eyes and clogged my throat. I shoved my hand against the screen and watched in satisfaction as it crashed to the ground.

Ethan propped the ladder against the house as Joe's squad car and the first fire truck roared into the drive. Firefighters grappled with hoses, scurrying across the yard like a swarm of ants. Shouts drifted to where I hung halfway out the window. Aunt Eunice and Uncle Roy rushed from their trucks, only to be held back by the fire crew.

April scampered down and sprinted to where Joe waited, his arms held wide. He gathered her close to him and rested his chin on the top of her head.

I smiled through my tears of relief at my savior and joined him, one arm held tight around a squirming Truly. "Joe must have called you." Once I planted my feet solidly on the ground, the dog leaped free.

He nodded. "I was closer than he was." Ethan pulled me to his chest. "I got here as fast as I could."

"You got here right on time." I wanted to stay wrapped in his arms, but a fireman insisted I follow him to his truck.

Huge plumes of projected water and chemicals made short work of the flames devouring the front porch. I assumed the back to be the same. At least they saved most of the house. The wraparound porch was a goner, and some of the siding showed scorch marks. I hated to think what would've happened if the fire department had taken longer to arrive.

Aunt Eunice bustled to where I sat on the bumper of the emergency vehicle. She clutched me to her bosom. I unburied my face. "I'm fine. Sorry about the house. I broke the front window."

"You silly goose. You're what's important."

Uncle Roy clapped me on the back. "The house will be fine. I'll build a new porch and buy a new window. You can't be replaced."

The firefighter strapped an oxygen mask to my face. *I must look a sight with all my scrapes and bruises, let alone smelling of smoke and wearing a mask.*

A fit of the giggles overtook me. I tried stifling them and ended up coughing. I pulled the mask from my face and waved the firefighter aside. "I'm fine."

"She's hysterical. She always acts like this when she's scared." Aunt Eunice peered into my face. "The strain's been too much for her."

Uncle Roy looked down his bifocals at me. "I think you're right." He turned back to the paramedic. "Give her a shot of something."

Their comments only served to increase my giggles. Ethan stood a few feet away, staring at me with his arms crossed. Then he stepped forward, grabbed my face in his hands, and kissed me. Not a brotherly peck. A long, breath-stealing, lip-smashing kiss.

The giggles stopped. And a fire burned in my stomach. I stared bug-eyed at his back as he stalked away. Who was this man, and what had he done with Ethan?

***

Once the firefighters, police, and paramedics had disappeared, Uncle Roy propped a panel of plywood over some cement blocks before he allowed me and Aunt Eunice to cross the burned, blackened porch and go into the house. Aunt Eunice took my arm and led me up the stairs as if I were an invalid.

Uncle Roy headed out to the shed and returned with a large roll of plastic sheeting, which he taped across the front window. Ethan watched the proceedings with hooded eyes.

Aunt Eunice supervised. Her brow wrinkled. "I'm not sleeping in a house with nothing between me and a killer but a sheet of plastic."

I plopped on the sofa and gathered my trembling dog to me. I should be trying to figure out who wanted to kill me, but my traitorous mind kept replaying Ethan's kiss. I ran a finger over my lips.

"Are you listening to me, Summer?" Aunt Eunice stood over me, her hands planted on her hips. "Is there something wrong with your lip? Did you burn it?"

"What?" My hand dropped to my side faster than a falling stone. "I didn't hear you."

"Obviously. I asked whether you felt safe sleeping in a house with plastic on the windows."

"Not really. But I'm too tired to drive twenty miles to a motel." And there was no way I'd stay at Ethan's house.

"I'll sit up with my shotgun. You ladies will be fine." Uncle Roy stomped upstairs, apparently to fetch the weapon.

Aunt Eunice plopped next to me. "What's on your mind, girlie? I can tell something is."

"I'm bothered by all the cars with the busted windshields."

"Were they similar or the same car?"

I shrugged. "You know me and cars."

Aunt Eunice tapped her bottom lip with her finger. "You should have said something at church. We could have asked somebody. Mabel's new Caddy has a broken windshield. Said a drunk tossed a bottle at it. So does Mrs. Hodge's old Continental."

"A man dragged Terri's body out of a large-model car."

"Mrs. Hodge has a son and a new beau. Could be Mabel has a man hiding in the wings, too. And then there's Duane Parker. He's been a rascal in the past."

"Do you know what he drives?"

"Duane drives a big old boat of a car."

I traded the dog for a cushy sofa pillow, wrapping my arms around the soft fleece. "Have you ever seen Mrs. Hodge's son? I didn't know she had one."

"I haven't seen that boy since he was a little bitty thing. Mrs. Hodge lived away until earlier this year." Aunt Eunice played with the hair around the dog's ears. "She did mention she didn't see much of Ricky."

"Mrs. Hodge mentioned that about her son to me, too."

I gnawed my lower lip as I replayed the conversation between April and me. Someone must have listened outside the kitchen window. Had we said anything of importance? I thought we'd only mentioned suspects, but. . . I jerked as someone barged into the room. *Ethan.*

"You scared us."

"Sorry." Ethan carried a sleeping bag over his shoulder, unrolled it under the plastic on the window, and stretched his frame on top of the bag.

"What are you doing?" I asked.

"I'm sleeping right here. Roy told me y'all weren't going anywhere, so I'm spending the night."

Ethan folded his arms beneath his head. His profile was chiseled. Determined and unbelievably handsome. His chin showed traces of soot. Blond curls, begging for my fingers, lay tousled around his head. I could see the boy the man had been. A boy with the face of an angel and the temperament of a scalawag. My heart went out to his mother. Well, the small part left over that didn't belong to him.

Uncle Roy pounded down the stairs, his rifle cradled in the crook of one arm. "I told you there ain't gonna be no man spending the night under this roof that ain't married to a woman under the same roof. Christian or not. I bent the rules the other night and didn't sleep a wink for it."

Ethan continued to stare at the ceiling, although I could detect the twinkle of a dimple near his mouth. "You and Eunice can chaperone. I'm staying, Roy. Accept it or shoot me."

I don't think I'd ever felt more frightened, or more elated, in my life. Uncle Roy waving his rifle around was scary. Accidents happened all the time. I didn't want the man I loved shot and killed.

The elation came from Ethan's willingness to take a bullet to protect me. I wanted to cry from sheer joy. I also wished for a bowl of popcorn. This scenario was better than any movie I'd ever seen.

"I'm not going to shoot you." The barrel of the gun dropped to point at the floor. "I'd already planned on sleeping down here. I guess two is better than one."

I got to my feet and planted a kiss on his weathered cheek. "I'm going upstairs, Uncle Roy. My virtue is safe with you around." I reached my room and realized this was the first night in several I didn't hear Duane's whistling. Had I heard it on the evening of our other break-ins?

18

Ethan nursed a coffee at the kitchen table, his large hands wrapped around the porcelain mug. The sun shone through the parted curtains, highlighting his hair with a halo of gold and casting his unshaved chin into a thatch of yellow fuzz. I'd swear I lost my breath at the sight of his gorgeousness. I clenched my fists, wanting to caress his cheek to feel the stubble.

A vision of a young tousle-headed boy copying the moves of his father appeared to me. My heart yearned for that boy to be my son. Ethan's and mine.

"Didn't sleep well?" I opened the refrigerator in hopes of spotting something for breakfast.

"Not really." There must have been something fascinating in his mug, because Ethan still hadn't raised his eyes. Definitely not a morning person. I made a mental note.

I grabbed a carton of orange juice. How did a woman talk to a man after a kiss like the one he'd given me. "Uh, thanks for staying last night."

"You aren't doing a very good job of looking out for yourself. I feel responsible for you, Summer, but it's like I'm fighting a losing battle trying to keep you safe."

I ran my tongue over my lips, unsure of how to respond. Was he serious, or was this another not-being-a-morning-person type of thing? The Bible says a kind word turns away wrath. "Well, thank you anyway."

And not being a morning person myself, I couldn't help but add, "But considering I'm still alive and kicking,

I'm not doing too bad a job of taking care of myself."

He raised his head, fixing me with a cold blue stare. I flinched. What happened to the golden boy? He'd frozen as solid as an iceberg. "And, uh, not that I'm not grateful or anything. I am. Really. You always show up when I need you, but I'm getting close to figuring out who the murderer is. That's the only reason someone is after me. Once they're behind bars, everything will be fine."

"You don't get it, do you?" Ethan rose, shaking his head. He glanced at me, his eyes hooded and filled with sadness. "Try to make it through the day, all right? I've got work to do."

I nodded, and he disappeared out the back door. That man was moodier than any woman I'd ever met. I lifted the orange juice to my lips.

Aunt Eunice marched in. "Don't drink out of the carton, Summer. I taught you better." She snatched it from my hands and poured the juice into a glass. "What did you say to Ethan to run him out of here? Man looked like he wanted to strangle a bear."

"I said thank you. That's all."

"Had to have been more." Aunt Eunice poured a glass for herself. "Are you coming to work today? I'm getting tired of running things myself."

"Have they hired anyone to take over the jewelry store yet?" A change of subject seemed wise. It wasn't as if I chose to be injured. To put myself in harm's way. Had I?

"I don't know what that has to do with the question I asked you, but I believe Mrs. Hodge is taking over. At least temporarily. Seems she's got some background in retail."

Really? "I'm going to grab my purse, and I'll be ready to go." My mind moved faster than my healing body. I must have looked like a ninety-year-old woman moving out of the room, every joint stiff and sore. If someone had listened closely, I'm sure they would've heard my bones creak.

~

Stress evaporated as I opened the door to the shop. Breathing the sweet aroma of chocolate soothed me.

I sat at the dipping machine, my mind drifting over the day's to-do list. During lunch, I wanted to visit the jewelry store to see Mrs. Hodge and, hopefully, her Continental. Same with Mabel's Cadillac. Although Ruby had moved to my number three suspect position because she wasn't driving a vehicle with a busted windshield, I still wanted to know where she'd gotten the rock on her finger.

Aunt Eunice passed the machine and grabbed the tray of dipped creams. She frowned. "I thought we made chocolate creams. According to your little swirl, these are vanilla."

"Oh no." I held out my arms to take the tray back. "I'll have to fix them. They are chocolate." *Lord, could we please solve this case? I need to get back to my life.*

"Must be thinking about the kiss Ethan planted on you last night." Aunt Eunice winked. "Worked better than a slap at shutting you up."

"You saw that?" The hated heat rose up my neck.

"Honey, everybody saw it." Aunt Eunice's cackle followed her to the storeroom.

My mind flashed to last night. The whirling red and blue lights. The sprinting firefighters decked out in fire gear. My hysterical giggles. Everyone staring at me. The kiss. The hoots and hollers.

I gasped. *Horror.* I'd pushed aside the hoots and hollers, believing, in my naïveté, that everyone cheered because they'd put out the fire. I lowered my head into my palm. *What a dope.*

"Embarrassed?" Aunt Eunice still laughed as she passed me on her way to the front of the store. "I thought we were going to have another fire to put out. That was a hot kiss. Red-hot." She fanned her face with her hand. "Steaming hot. I'll tell you who else was steaming—your uncle Roy. I thought he was going to shoot that boy right then and there." She clutched her side. "Then when Ethan announced he planned on staying the night. . . Whoo-ee. I haven't had that much excitement in years."

"That's enough, Aunt Eunice." The bell over the door saved me. *Thank the Lord.* Aunt Eunice waddled, doubled over, snorting her amusement. A customer occupied her, so I grasped the opportunity to leave. I yelled that I would be back in a half hour. Then I snatched my purse from a nearby hook and ducked out the rear.

I had laid claim to a set of keys for Aunt Eunice's truck, and although I didn't enjoy driving a stick shift without power steering, the Chevy was all that was available. First stop, the jewelry store.

Being as stiff as I was, it had take a Herculean feat to climb behind the wheel, but being determined, I gritted my teeth and hauled myself in. I had no desire to walk the few blocks to the store. Not unless someone wanted to carry me back.

I turned the key three times before the engine sputtered to life, and I pulled slowly out of the alley, expecting Aunt Eunice to come charging out to stop me. I should have asked to take her baby, but she'd told me I could drive the truck anytime I wanted to. I didn't want to; I needed to.

Mountain Shadows wasn't a big city by certain standards, but come lunchtime, cars flooded the streets. It took several minutes before traffic cleared enough for me to drive from my alley to the one across Main Street. The less I used the surface streets, the less chance of something happening to the Chevy.

I spotted the back of Shadow Jewelers. Mrs. Hodge's black Continental sat shining like an onyx, washed, waxed, and complete with a busted windshield.

Not set up for parking, the alley had limited options. I could drive around front, but I didn't want to give my neighbor warning, just in case she was the guilty party. I chose a space between the Continental and the brick wall of another building.

After shutting off the engine, I cracked open my door. There wasn't enough space. Now I remembered why I hadn't driven this big boat of a truck before.

No way I'd fit through the few inches allowed. I glanced to my right. Nope. Too close. I should have parked in the delivery spot in front of the door. I groaned and restarted the engine, preparing my retreat, when April's car pulled behind me and stopped horizontal to the truck, blocking my exit.

"Hey!" I laid on the horn and glared in my rearview mirror. I opened the truck window. "April, get out of the way! I'm trying to back up." Her tinted windows were shut. Funny, the shape of the person inside didn't look like April.

Her front door opened.

"April—"

My heart stopped as a man in a ski mask exited. This wasn't April. I rolled up my window as he walked toward the truck. I turned in my seat. He sauntered as close to the driver's side door as he could squeeze, eyes glittering from the slits of a ski mask. His lips curled into a grin. I don't know how long we stared at each other. Long enough for my lungs to hurt from the breath I held.

I released it and reached for my cell phone. He watched while I flipped the cover to dial the police. *Oh no!* I'd forgotten to charge the phone last night. But I couldn't let him suspect anything.

Using my index finger, I pushed buttons, holding the phone so he could see me calling 911. The man held up a paper on which he'd written the words, "Give it up." Then he gave a wave and strode down the alley, leaving me boxed in.

Give it up? Was he crazy? I had no choice now but to pursue this case I'd started. My Irish stubbornness demanded this be finished. Clearly, we played a game of cat and mouse. Well, I wouldn't be an easy mouse to capture. Even though I sat trapped in the cab of a truck that was quickly reaching an uncomfortably hot temperature.

The man paused at the end of the alley.

I rolled down my window. "I have no intention of giving up anything. Show yourself like a man."

He turned his masked face toward me and took a step in my direction. Heart pounding, I rolled up my window faster than I could tell myself what a doofus I was. The man spun around and left.

"Summer, you're a dodo head. If your Irish temper doesn't get you killed, your own stupidity will." I leaned against the back of the seat to catch my breath. "Lord, thank You for watching out for the foolish ones, of which I am queen."

Glancing in the rearview mirror, I tried judging the distance between the truck's bumper and the brick wall of the store. The truck could knock the car sideways, but there wasn't enough room to get any momentum. I was stuck.

I unhooked my seat belt and rolled down my window. Slinging my purse around my neck, I got to my knees, positioning myself so my behind rested on the window frame. I thanked God I hadn't worn a dress.

Wiggling into an unnatural position, I was sure I resembled a broken pretzel. I finally got my head free of the truck and wall, then squirmed until my body followed. Bracing my back, I "walked" myself out of the truck and jumped to the ground. Even being double-jointed, my body sported some new aches and pains.

I peered around the corner, expecting the masked stranger to reappear. *Nope.* I transferred my attention to the abandoned vehicle. I stomped around the Toyota and pounded on the back door of Shadow Jewelers. Within minutes, Mrs. Hodge opened the door, a bemused look on her face.

"Summer?" She craned her neck to peer around me. "Why didn't you come in through the front?"

I chose not to answer and turned to point at the cars. "Someone purposely blocked me in. I had to climb out the truck window."

"You poor thing." She clucked her tongue and stepped aside. "Come on in. I'll get you a glass of ice water."

I followed her into the welcome coolness of the air-conditioned reception area. She ducked into a small kitchen, leaving me alone. The rear of the store sat in gloom. No light spilled in from the customer area. "Are you open? I really need to use a phone."

Mrs. Hodge reappeared, shrugged, then handed me the water. "Sure, you can use the phone. I'll get it for you in just a sec. I'm still getting myself acquainted as to where everything is. It's been so long since I've worked, you know."

I lifted the glass to my lips. Thinking back over the last few days and how someone had been out to get me, I lowered the water without drinking. "Why'd you take the job? I mean, there must be plenty of younger people looking for work."

"It's only part-time, and I've little enough to do. Aren't you thirsty?"

I pretended to drink. "Mrs. Hodge, may I ask you something?"

"Sure, honey."

"Is your car window busted?"

19

My window's broke?"

For an elderly woman, Mrs. Hodge was as spry as a puppy. She sprinted to the back door and yanked it open. I didn't need my trusty *Dolt's Guide* to know I'd hit on something of importance. Mrs. Hodge made all the right movements, but her facial expressions weren't convincing. My news hadn't surprised her.

I decided to play along with her charade. I set the glass on the nearest counter and followed her outside.

Mrs. Hodge stood wringing her hands, face wrinkled with concern. "Who would do this?"

I wonder. "You didn't notice the crack when you drove into work this morning?" The crack was more like a shatter, a spider webbing its way across the windshield.

"I think I would've noticed something like that, don't you?" She stepped closer to the vehicle.

"So, it happened after you got to work?" I sounded like a bona fide investigator.

"I said so, didn't I?" Mrs. Hodge turned to glare at me. "Is something bothering you?"

"No. I guess we'll have to call the police about your window and my aunt's truck. Can we use the phone in the store?" I had to admit, Mrs. Hodge put on an Academy Award–winning performance—the wringing of hands and injured attitude, complete with under-the-breath mutterings. She could be innocent, I suppose. I'd know more after interviewing Mabel.

The receptionist at the police department said Joe

was on his way. I ducked across the street for a soda. With Mrs. Hodge being a potential murderer, or an accessory, I didn't feel safe drinking anything she gave me. A professional investigator would more than likely tell me not to leave a suspect unsupervised, but my throat felt as parched as Mountain Shadows had during the drought last summer.

Several people stared at me as I waited in line for my drink. One handed me a business card for a women's crisis shelter. Remembering my colorful bruises, I almost explained about meeting the tree. The old Summer would have. She spoke with anyone who spoke back. The new Summer tried to be more refined, like the verse in Proverbs that says a wise man holds his tongue, or something to that effect. Maybe it was a wise man ponders his words. Either way, I wasn't going to blab to every soul I met.

Slurping happily on my straw, I headed at a snail's pace back to the jewelers'. I arrived as Joe and another officer pulled up. The officer looked about as old as a high school graduate. Had to be a rookie.

The three of us entered the store. Mrs. Hodge hung up the phone and gave us a thin smile. She folded her hands in front of her. "Officers."

"Mrs. Hodge." Joe removed his hat. "May we see the vehicle?"

"That'll be rather difficult, Officer." Mrs. Hodge fell into a rolling chair. "It's gone."

The other officer, whom Joe still hadn't introduced, lifted a pen from his notepad. He raised a questioning gaze to Joe.

"Where is it?" Joe donned his "cop" face, which

always cracked me up. He set his chin firmly and pursed his lips, bugged his eyes and stared with intensity, as if he were trying to see through a person. I bit my bottom lip to keep from smiling.

"Well." Mrs. Hodge fidgeted, crossing and uncrossing her ankles. "After Summer left to get a drink, I heard this horrible racket in the alley. I thought about checking it out, but I was afraid. When the noise quit, I took a peek. Someone moved the car blocking Summer's truck, and my car had disappeared."

Officer Unknown's pen raced across his pad of paper. I tried craning my neck to see what he'd written, but he caught me staring and turned around.

"Let's take a look." Joe slapped on his hat and led us to where April's Toyota sat smashed against the wall of the store. Tire tracks left easy-to-read signs that another vehicle had been there. The Continental was nowhere in sight.

"April's going to cry." Joe pounded his thigh. "She reported the car stolen this morning."

She did love that car. It was the first automobile April ever owned, and she'd paid it off three months ago. "At least Aunt Eunice's truck is okay." The red monster sat exactly where I'd left it. I planted my hands on my hips. "My guess is, someone came with a tow truck, moved April's car, and hauled the Continental away."

Joe stared at me for probably a full minute before he rolled his eyes.

"I'm not finished, Mr. Smarty-Pants Cop Man." I called him what I'd taunted him with as a kid when we'd played cops and robbers. I lowered my voice. "There's no way Mrs. Hodge didn't know what was going on. Did you notice she hung up the phone when we got back? She seemed nervous, too. The line at the diner took about twenty minutes, with it being lunchtime and all. Someone could've done this in that amount of time. Don't you think? When they blocked me inside the truck, it took less than that amount of time for me to wiggle myself free."

"Good observation." He scowled at me. "And we'll have to talk more about you being blocked in. It's amazing how much information you tend to leave out. I also think we need to take Mrs. Hodge to the station for questioning."

I saluted my cousin. "My job here is done. I'm going to visit Mabel now. I'll talk to you later." Now that the Continental was gone, I could open the passenger's side door of the truck and slide behind the wheel.

"Summer."

"I know. Be careful." I waved out the rear window as I backed the truck out of the tight space. "Bye."

Erring on the side of caution, I parked out front of the newspaper building, right next to Mabel's black Cadillac. No way I'd chance getting blocked in again. I glanced at my watch and winced that I'd been gone over an hour. Aunt Eunice would kill me. I pushed open the revolving glass door of the newspaper office.

Mabel sat behind the reception desk, a mug of coffee in one hand and a women's magazine in the other. "Hello, Summer. Your face looks bad. Does it hurt much?"

I leaned my elbows on the counter. "Not a bit."

"Need something?" She sipped her coffee.

"I was driving by and noticed the window's broken on your new Cadillac. What happened?"

Mabel choked, spewing coffee over the pages of

her magazine. Her lips disappeared as she pressed them together. Probably in an attempt not to hurt me. She picked up the magazine with two fingers and shook it over the floor. Brown drops of liquid flew across the tile.

"A rock."

"Must've been a big rock." I thought my face would crack with the effort to hold back the smile threatening to burst forth. She'd all but admitted to being a liar.

"Good sized. Silly kids playing a makeshift game of baseball. Minus the ball." Mabel spread the magazine across the dry section of the desk. She folded her hands and peered at me over her glasses. "Why are you asking me these questions? Sounds like you're fishing for something. If you are, spit it out. I'm busy."

I debated whether I should be up-front with her. Put her on her guard. I never could hide anything from the woman. Not since I was a child.

"Will this be off the record?"

Mabel leaned back. "If you want it to."

"The other night, someone contacted me about giving them something they thought I had. We set up a place to meet. They tried to run me over. I busted their windshield with a rock about the size of a baseball."

"And you think that someone was me?" Mabel threw her head back and guffawed. "That's priceless, girl! I heard all about Terri Lee's body being dumped at your feet." She held up her arm like a weightlifter showing off a bicep. "Yahoo! I'm still young enough for someone to think I can lift a human body that weighs more than three pounds."

My skin betrayed me in its usual way, sending heat up my neck. "It was a man who dumped her body." *How'd she know? Aunt Eunice?* They told each other everything.

Mabel snorted, trying to get her laughter under control. "You are priceless, girl. Truly priceless."

"Good-bye, Mabel." I stiffened my back, spun, and marched out the door. *How rude.*

Aunt Eunice stood on the sidewalk in front of the candy store, hands on her hips. She looked both ways. I'm surprised her glare didn't shatter the truck's windshield.

"Sorry, Aunt Eunice. You won't believe the day I've had."

"Try me." Her eyes widened to the point where I wondered whether they pained her as I retold the happenings of the last hour.

"Don't you worry none about Mabel, Summer. I told you she wasn't a killer, but if it's that important to you, I'll find out what happened to her window."

"She said a rock. Find out if she knows who threw it." I followed her into the store and stashed my purse under the counter. "I can't believe someone would bash April's car. If they'd already stolen it once, why not just drive it away?"

"Sounds like they didn't have a lot of time to spare." Aunt Eunice motioned her head toward the phone. "Call Joe. He said it was important."

Great. Maybe he'd discovered something. Anything to help solve this. "Did Ethan call?"

"No, expecting him to?"

I shrugged.

"Man's busy doing God's work. Fulfilling his calling as a woodworking teacher. Something you need to figure out. Find out what God's call for your life is. It might keep you out of trouble. Ethan'll call when he gets a chance." She bent to lower the flame on the gas stove.

What was God's will for me? Did I want to know? I reached for the phone and punched in Joe's direct line.

"Joe Parson."

"You called?" I perched on the stool.

"Do you know a Richard Bland?"

I studied my fingernails. Definitely in desperate need of a manicure. "I've heard the name. Wait a minute." I straightened, my mind racing. What was the name April had given me? "He's the missing diamond broker. Why?"

"We found his fingerprints on Terri Lee's body."

"That doesn't make sense, Joe. Why wouldn't he wear gloves? And where's he been hiding all this time? Does he think we won't catch him?"

"I don't know. It was only a partial print. We're lucky to have found it at all. Keep your busybody ears open. You are cooperating with the police, right?"

I rolled my eyes. "Yes, I'm cooperating with the police. But I don't really care for Officer Wayne. He doesn't keep in touch very well. He never calls me with an update."

"He doesn't have to." *Click.*

I couldn't believe Joe had hung up on me. I donned my apron, washed my hands, and rushed to help Aunt Eunice mix the concoction for the chocolate-covered cherries. If I didn't mix the ingredients quickly enough, the sugar would harden. Once we'd finished mixing, we scraped the coating into a bucket, covered it with a damp dish towel, and snapped on the airtight lid. The two of us moved like a well-oiled machine, anticipating the other's movements. Once again I prayed for a speedy solving of this case. Making candy didn't raise my blood pressure as much as trying to stay alive.

Despite the bruises and marks even makeup couldn't hide, I had to be honest: I was enjoying myself. I had no idea what investigating this case would entail, but it was definitely a wild ride.

I lined up candy paper cups in a nine-by-thirteen-inch pan as I perused the list of nut clusters I had to make. Cashews again? "Aunt Eunice, you using the milk or the dark chocolate?"

"Whichever."

I chose the milk, solely because I loved the color. The deep, satiny sheen. I lifted the spoon and held it high, watching as the liquid poured in a glorious stream. Gazing at chocolate as it melted and swirled in the pan helped me think. It was almost hypnotic.

I caught Aunt Eunice watching me and replaced the spoon.

"Summer"—she sat across the scarred wooden table, dropping dippers of dark chocolate onto the slab in front of her—"pay attention. You're miles away."

"I was thinking of ways to kill someone with chocolate. If you were to drown in it—literally, I mean—would you mind? We're talking about chocolate here."

"Good heavens!"

"Well?"

"I guess not. If I had to pick between drowning in anything or chocolate, I'd definitely pick chocolate."

"Me, too."

"This case getting to you?"

"Yes." My shoulders slumped. "I had every intention of devoting myself to this store completely. Instead, you're the one who's been running things. I pop in now and then to make candy, but that's about it."

"And? I know there's something you're not telling me."

"And sometimes Ethan seems interested in me. Protective. More like a lover than a friend. At other times, he treats me like I'm a nuisance."

"You're more than a nuisance to him." Aunt Eunice stood and picked up her tray. "That man cares for you more than anything. I can see it in his eyes when he doesn't think anyone is looking. Be patient." She headed toward the refrigerator. "Leave the tray there and take out the garbage, would you? I'll finish up here. Then we can get home."

"Sounds great." I headed to the sink, washed my hands, unplugged my cell phone from where I'd left it charging, and slid it into the pocket of my apron. Its weight banging against my thigh would help me remember to take it home.

The garbage was heavy, and after I'd tugged the plastic bag from the bin, I slung it over my shoulder like Santa's bag of toys. I grunted under its weight. Aunt Eunice ran circles around me, and she was thirty years older.

Using my hip, I pushed the back door open then allowed the weight of the bag to carry me through. I tripped, landing on my knees. Pebbles poked through the thin fabric of my pants, sending sharp stabs of pain up my leg. The garbage bag broke open, and its contents spilled around me.

Bracing my hands under me, I started to push to my feet, but a blow to my head knocked me back. Asphalt pressed into my cheek. The alley tilted sideways. My vision blurred.

The world closed in and faded to black.

20

My nose caught a whiff of something musty. I sneezed, and my head pounded. Someone had stuffed something foul in my mouth, preventing my sneeze from going anywhere. I opened my eyes to nothing. A blanket of darkness engulfed me in a cocoon of fear. I tried to stretch my arms and legs. No room. A rope of some kind cut off the circulation in my wrists. Curled into a fetal position, I lay still. *Think, Summer. Think your way out of here.*

I shoved my tongue against the offending object. The cloth was rough yet slimy, and I gagged. It remained in place. Where was I? I remembered taking out the garbage and tripping. Then someone hit me in the back of the head with something. Aunt Eunice must be frantic by now. I squirmed, jerking like a hooked worm, and got absolutely nowhere.

Panting, I told myself to calm down. *Concentrate.* My chest rose and fell like the ocean during a hurricane. *One, two, three...* I struggled to regulate my breathing. I detested small spaces. My breath hissed through my nostrils.

I hated the dark. Ever since I'd got lost in the woods when I was eight. But to be trussed up like a turkey and left alone was more than I could bear. Fear, cold and suffocating, weighed me down.

God, help me. I wanted to feel Ethan's kiss bruising my lips. In love or anger, I didn't care at this point. He could tell me what to do whenever he wanted. I'd try to listen. I would.

Tears poured down my cheeks, burning a trail over

my skin. Then anger joined the terror, and I screamed beneath my gag, bucking my body up and down until exhaustion overtook me. My wrists bled onto whatever my captor bound me with.

I lay there sobbing. Was this where my life would end up? Hidden and tied in a—what? Where was I?

I rubbed my hands back and forth, feeling the rough fibers of carpet. Rolling from side to side took less than two rolls, and my knees knocked against something hard. Like metal. *The trunk of a car!* From the odor emanating under me, it was an old car.

Something scraped from outside my prison. Sounded like the crunching of pebbles. Footsteps?

I howled, sounding more like an injured bloodhound than a woman in trouble. Whoever waited outside banged on the trunk. My howl turned to a yelp, and I cringed, shrinking as small as possible.

Okay, no help there. I racked my brain for a solution to the latest dilemma I'd managed to get myself into. I came up with nothing until a still, small voice spoke to my heart telling me to call on Him.

I'm sorry, God. Once again I tried doing things on my own. Not stopping to ask for Your help. Well, I'm asking now. Please show me a way out of this.

My eyes strained through the murky darkness. They adjusted enough for me to make out a faint glow emanating through the cracked taillight. Night had fallen. A full moon cast shadows. I could distinguish the tall weeds and rocks of a rarely traveled dirt road.

Instinct told me my captor planned to leave me. Alone. Undiscovered. My temper flew to the surface. Not if I had anything to say about it. I didn't think it was part of God's plan for an old rusty car to be my coffin. Armed with His strength, I got to work.

I tightened into a ball at the pace of a snail, taking care not to make a loud noise. I couldn't tell whether my captor stood guard or not. I didn't want to pop the trunk and face some maniac ready to bash in my skull with a crowbar. My head hurt enough, thank you very much.

Curled like a roly-poly bug, I slid my arms down and around my bound legs until my tied hands were in front of me. *Thank You, God.* My captor used frayed rope. Obviously not a big fan of television. Any dummy knows you secure a prisoner with zip ties now. Truly had been secured with zip ties. Was it the same person? Why use something different on me?

No longer tied up like a pig ready for roasting, I lifted my hands and ripped the tape holding my gag. I stifled the scream threatening to erupt.

Imitating a rodent gnawing on a ball of string, I chewed the rope. Fibers tasting of oil stuck to my tongue. I spat and rubbed my hands along the sides of my prison, searching for something sharp. *Ouch!* A piece of metal stuck out near my head. I positioned my arms and sawed furiously. By the time I'd finished, my muscles ached. I tried stretching, but even my small frame didn't leave much room. Escape was hard work. If I managed to free myself, I doubted I'd be able to take more than two steps. Except for the rapid rise and fall of my chest, I could be a corpse.

I was determined not to be.

I don't know how long it took to free my hands, but my neck throbbed when I'd finished. Rope fibers still stuck in my teeth. Curling back into a curved position,

I started on the ropes around my ankles, a more difficult job. I needed to feel my way, stretching my arms longer than they wanted to go. My shoulder cramped up in no time.

Please, God, this is taking too long. What if the person comes back? I can't last until morning. Alone. In the dark. You know I'm nothing but a big chicken.

In a final burst of strength, I scraped the rope over my ankles, hissing at the pain searing them. Yep, I'd left my DNA behind. I hoped it was enough for a search party to confirm the skin as mine.

The burning sensation abated, and I bruised my elbow knocking the backseat of the car flat. Who was the genius who first called it the funny bone? Nothing funny about hitting it. I opened the backseat door, crawled out, and took a deep breath of freedom.

The serenade of locusts and bullfrogs greeted me. The sky filled with roiling clouds. I couldn't call the twin tire tracks through the weeds a road in any aspect. It resembled the path the Headless Horseman might have traveled through a shadowy forest. My heart skipped a beat.

I glanced from side to side, wondering which way to go. *Okay, Lord, help me again.* Isn't it amazing how we turn to Him automatically when we're in trouble? I vowed to be different if I escaped these haunted woods in one piece. A chill came over me, and I shoved my hands into the pockets of my apron.

My cell phone! Hallelujah! I'd forgotten. Quicker than the lightning bolts streaking across the sky, my finger punched in Ethan's speed dial number.

"Ethan. Thank You, Lord. You've got to help me.

Someone's kidnapped me."

"Summer, where are you? We've been frantic." My insides melted, knowing how frightened he was.

I studied the path again then stared into the treetops. It was like trying to peer through ink. "I don't know. It's pitch-black, and there's nothing here. I'm standing on a road that's off the beaten path."

"Are you okay?"

"My elbow hurts, and I've scraped my wrists and ankles, maybe bleeding. Someone hit me over the head, tied me up, gagged me with a nasty cloth, and threw me in the trunk of a car. Ethan, I don't think I've ever been more frightened than I am now. What if they come back to kill me?"

"Look, stay on the phone. Joe is trying to—" *Click.*

Great. I glanced at my phone. I'd lost service. Wouldn't you know it? I tried dialing Ethan again. Nothing. Okay. Alone again. *Oops, sorry, Lord. I'm never alone. How soon I forget. But this sure is a forlorn-looking place.* I prayed there would be a way for Joe to trace my location.

I froze. Why hadn't my captor taken the phone? Hope sprang. Had they been interrupted? Maybe Aunt Eunice had yelled out to see what took me so long. *Thank You, Lord, for small favors.*

The Bible tells us the correct path isn't always the easiest. I chose the path the car appeared to have come from. I stared through the dark, trying to determine the model of the automobile. An Impala? I hadn't seen one in years. I darted to the driver's side and peered in. No keys.

I turned back and studied the trail. If the car had trouble coming down this poor excuse for a road, going back in the direction it came from made sense to me.

Agony hit me with every step. I thought I'd been sore earlier in the day. Or was it yesterday? A vacation compared to this. Crawling out of the car and walking for what seemed like an hour gave me a good idea what the word *excruciating* meant. My wrists and ankles stung like the fury of fire ant bites. The bottoms of my feet throbbed. My shoulders felt permanently warped. Stooped. Cemented there with a glue called pain.

I plopped on the ground, leaning back against a fallen log. I wanted an ice-cold diet cola. I wanted to plunge my hands, wrist deep, into a pan of warm melted chocolate. I wanted an air conditioner. I plucked my sweaty blouse away from my body. Why did someone have to kidnap me in July? The hottest month in the Ozark foothills. The air was so thick I could almost quench my thirst.

I wished for autumn and juicy muscadine grapes. Even nasty persimmons. Pecans, huckleberries, anything safe to eat. I bolted to my feet. *Please tell me I haven't been sitting in poison ivy. Wouldn't that make my day?*

I checked the phone reception again. Nothing. Sliding my aching feet along the weed-grown path, I moved like a zombie, moaning and swinging my arms. I exaggerated the swings until I giggled, picturing myself looking like an intoxicated gorilla.

Admit it, Summer. You have no idea where you are or where you're headed, and you're losing your mind.

I stopped. I could tell from the shade of darkness the night was late. Early morning, more likely. My eyelids grew heavy, and my head ached. I felt the goose egg above my neck.

Summer, you might as well sit down and give it up. The hard ground met my rear end abruptly. Add one more body part to my list of hurts. A fun movement that sent me down a small hill. I folded my arms over my knees. When I reached the bottom, I lowered my head and cried.

To make matters worse, storm clouds were about to release their wares in a torrent. My clothes clung to my body. I panted in the thick air. Lightning zigzagged across the sky, followed by booms of thunder.

I lifted my tear-raw face to the heavens. The first big raindrop plopped in the center of my forehead. Within minutes, Mountain Shadows' drought ended. The hard, cracked ground ran beneath a ton of water.

I'd chosen to rest in a place now sitting under at least an inch of water. *Great.* I'd decided to have my breakdown in a dried creek bed. Soon I'd find myself in a precarious situation. I snorted. As if the situation I'd been in all day wasn't bad enough.

I scrambled up the sides of the shallow wash, ducking as the sky lit up like an exploding flashbulb. My scream joined the cymbal crash of the thunder. The top of a mountain during a July thunderstorm wasn't a safe place to be. Not with lightning dancing across the sky. How did the valley fare? Had Uncle Roy patched the hole in the roof?

Once I'd pulled my aching, soaked, and now muddy self back to the path, I hobbled down it. It would be safer to keep moving. The road started somewhere.

The wet apron chafed my neck. I removed it and tied it around my waist. The worthless cell phone banged against my thigh, taunting me. Reminding me of its uselessness.

Weeds and bushes dripping with rain slapped against my legs, pressing, for just a second, with each pass. With the humidity, I was as wet inside as out. I wanted to be home. I wanted Ethan to wrap his arms around me. I didn't care if the loving came with a lecture or not.

As the sun's rays peeked their first glorious light over the horizon, I stumbled—literally—onto the road. I landed on my knees, scraping my palms. *What's one more scrape?* Struggling to get back on my feet, I allowed a grin to spread across my face. I'd made it. I had no idea which road I'd fallen upon, and I didn't care. I was out of the woods.

Tired and out of sorts, I lowered myself to the ground beneath a thick bush and made a seat in a patch of wet pine needles. Sometime during the early morning hours, I slept to the lullaby of falling raindrops.

Rain still fell when I awoke to the sun's full light. Shivering, I pushed to my feet and crawled from beneath the bush.

No longer under the shelter of the trees, I stood in the center of the road, arms outstretched, and twirled. I opened my mouth like a starving baby bird, allowing the abating rain to fall on my face and tongue. *Thank You, Lord.*

I lowered my arms and surveyed the road. I turned left, hoping it would lead me down the mountain. Being so early in the morning, I experienced a moment of surprise when a car appeared over the hill to my right. I stepped away from the center of the road.

"Summer?" Nate barked before the car came to a complete halt. He opened the door and leaped from the car. "Where have you been? Most of the town is looking for you."

"Oh, hanging around up here. You know, Mother Nature and all." I allowed him to place a ratty old blanket from his backseat around my shoulders. "Thank God you chose to look for me up here. I thought I'd have to walk back to town." The man might be a nuisance, one I didn't feel completely safe around, but he was a familiar face.

Nate helped me into the car and closed the door. Back behind the wheel, he turned to me. "Good thing. You were headed farther up, not down."

"Really?" I could have sworn. "Well, thank you anyway." I shrugged.

He put the car in gear and pulled away. "Anytime."

Nate's demeanor changed. Cold. I couldn't see the soft, in-love-with-me man anywhere in his hard profile. A muscle twitched in his jaw.

I bent down to examine my ankle and disturbed a stack of papers. At my feet sat a box of Summer Confections chocolate fudge. *Wonderful.* I was starving. I opened the box and gasped. Instead of fudge, diamonds winked up at me.

21

My heart stopped. I bolted to an upright position, peering from out of the corner of my eye at Nate's face. A smirk twisted one corner of his lips. "You found my jewels. There ought to be more where those came from, but alas, they've been misplaced."

Jewels? As in diamonds? "You're Richard Bland, aren't you?" I tugged the blanket tighter, warding off the chill from the car's air conditioner. It all made sense. New to town, knew his diamonds. Mrs. Hodge's son had been gone then suddenly came back into the picture. I stared out the window into the continuing drizzle, my heart a cold stone in my chest. Shivers of fear took over my body. "Ricky." The pieces fell into place. "You're Mrs. Hodge's son. The two of you aren't estranged."

He shook a finger in my face. "And you're too clever for your own good. But we are estranged. Can you believe, my dear mother wasn't happy to see me after all these years? But after a bit of persuasion, she agreed to play along with my scheme."

Nate twisted a hand in my hair and shoved my face into the dashboard. Stars swam before my eyes. The lights went out.

When I came to, Nate had slung me over his shoulder like a sack of potatoes. My head hung down his back. Remembering something I'd read about self-defense, I kicked in earnest, aiming for anything that would hurt.

"Oh no, you don't." He wrapped his arm tighter around my knees.

Self-defense classes moved to the top of my to-do list. "Put me down."

"I don't think that would be wise. Not until we're inside." Keeping his hold on me, he stomped up a set of rickety wooden steps. Keys jangled in his hand.

He deposited me inside what, on some slim imagination, someone might call a house. We stood on warped wooden boards over two-by-fours. The roof leaked, raindrops hitting the floor with dull plops. Boards covered the windows, and I could see the gray light of a rainy day through the walls.

"Nice place. Been here long?" I plopped on the tattered plaid sofa, sending dust into the air.

Nate chuckled. "I do like you, Summer Meadows. You're good for a laugh." He lifted his shirt and pulled a revolver from the waistband of his pants. I wanted to kick myself for not checking when I had a glimpse of his backside.

"Gee, thanks. I'm thrilled." I clutched the blanket tighter around my shoulders. "Going to kill me now?"

"I don't want to." He sounded like a little boy whose mommy had told him to go to bed. "If only you hadn't found those diamonds. Hadn't started poking your pretty little nose where it didn't belong. I knew you'd figure it out sooner or later."

A nervous giggle escaped me. "You planted them beneath my rosebush. It was only a matter of time, Nate."

"I didn't plant them there!"

"Who did? Terri Lee?"

"Stupid woman." Nate paced a section of floor where two boards lay side by side.

"She said she had to hurry. Someone was coming. That ex-con Parker and his stupid nightly strolls. Did you know the man walks the highway at night? In the dark, no less? Terri tried convincing me she'd left enough evidence to put suspicion on him." He whirled to face me.

"But why did she hide the diamonds there and then put the cash in your tree house? She tried to stiff me, that's why. I killed her boyfriend. She'd told him too much. Then when she found out Parker worked in a nursery where they sold gloves along with everything else, she stuck that glove under the rosebush. She tried to frame me. She wanted things to point to me if someone found the diamonds before she could get them. And when the DNA comes back with that dead guy's blood on there, with something I'd left behind. . ." Nate's mouth twisted.

I shrugged. Something about Nate had always bothered me. Even when I almost turned to him instead of Ethan. Now I knew what it was. He was nuts. His attention had charmed me, though, and it hurt that he'd used me in order to find his precious diamonds.

The cell phone in my pocket vibrated. Sliding my right hand beneath the blanket, I pressed the ON button.

"I had plans, Summer. Plans to get out of here. Plans on helping Mom." He waved the gun around before bending to peer at me. "Terri was going to swindle me out of my share. Can you believe it? I was the one who stole the diamonds. I was the one who came up with my new identity. Not her." He straightened.

"Why'd you have Terri as a partner at all, Nate? You could've had the diamonds and the cash all to yourself. Why share?" I needed to keep him talking. *Please, God, let Ethan be on the other end of my phone.* "You could have. You're Richard Bland, the supposed diamond broker."

He snorted. "That was just a story I spread around town to get the focus off me. Terri Lee was the connection. She wasn't hard to get close to. She was the most man-hungry woman I've ever met. I'm plain old Richard Hodge, the thorn in my dear mother's side."

"Being man-hungry isn't a reason for murder. What about Terri Lee's boyfriend?"

"He was in the way. Getting too close. I could see Terri Lee turning. Wanting someone young and handsome. Then I saw you. A fiery temptress, and Terri didn't seem important anymore."

Had Nate ever looked in the mirror? I mean, he didn't appear handsome at the moment. Not with his features twisted in hate, but I couldn't remember having seen a prettier man before. Except for my Ethan.

"So you did kill her. You dumped her beneath the overhang where I waited."

"Yep, that was me. I knew you didn't have the diamonds. I'm not stupid. That oaf of a cousin of yours has them. I knew they wouldn't turn them over to me. I just wanted to have a little fun with the police." He stopped pacing and plopped next to me. I pulled away from him as he slung his arm along the back of the sofa.

"Why'd you tear up my room? Why hide the knife in my mattress?"

Nate sighed. "Foolishness. I was looking for the cash. You came home. I had to hide it somewhere and get out. If I was discovered, it'd be easier to come up with a story of why I was there if I wasn't wielding a weapon. I never would have guessed you'd do anything with the mattress except toss it out."

"I know you killed Terri Lee, but what about Doris?"

Nate smirked. "Annoying woman. She simply got in the way. Doris saw me pick up Terri Lee from work. Since that was the last time anyone saw the beautiful Terri Lee, I knew the woman would put two and two together."

He stopped and looked at me. "You know, Summer, you and I could be something. I could come up with another plan. We could run off to Europe and live the high life."

As if. "You aren't going to shoot me?"

"Haven't decided. That depends on you." His arm fell to my shoulders. "Of course, you'd have to give up that pious attitude of yours. I won't lavish wealth on you without getting something in return."

"You want me to bargain with sexual favors to stay alive?" I bolted off the sofa. "Shoot me now, Nate, because you won't get that from me."

"Don't tell me you really are hung up on the goody-goody man?" Nate's, or should I say Richard's, laugh rang through the room.

I scanned for anywhere to sit than beside him. "Where are we?"

"A place I've been staying in. If Terri Lee hadn't tricked me, I'd have been living in splendor. Maybe up in Little Rock, until I could get away. Maybe Hot Springs, or I could've headed up to Branson." He grabbed my hand. "Come with me. We'll go now. Sell your podunk candy store and come with me."

"No." I yanked my hand free. "I love Ethan, Nate. Always have, always will. Either let me go or kill me." What was I doing? *Lord, save me from myself. I don't want to die. I want another of Ethan's mouth-bruising kisses.*

"It's Richard. Richard Nathan Hodge. Keep it straight."

Ethan, are you getting all this? "Sorry. Are we still on the mountain?"

"I'm tired of talking." He lunged at me. "Let's have some fun before I decide what to do with you."

The man seemed to sprout six more arms. I stepped away from him. *Help me, God.* I'd be no match for him if he got ahold of me.

The floor gave way, and I crashed down several feet into what I assumed was once a storm cellar or underground pantry. I landed unhurt in a heap. Not exactly the type of rescuing I had in mind, but it had worked in a pinch.

Richard cursed and stood staring at me. "Give me your hand."

"No."

"Summer, give me your hand." He knelt beside the hole and held out his free hand.

I pressed myself against the farthest dirt wall. "No."

My heart stopped when my phone beeped. I must have hit a button as I fell.

"What is that? Do you have a cell phone in your pocket?" Richard let loose a stream of curses so vile I covered my ears.

"Fine!" He spun and disappeared from sight.

"Richard?"

Thunder crashed. Cold mud collected under my feet, and I stared with wide eyes overhead where a steady stream of rain poured in. I dug into my pocket, retrieved my phone, and stepped aside to avoid as much of the deluge as I could.

I punched in Ethan's speed dial number. "Ethan? Did you call earlier? Did you hear?"

"Summer. Thank God. Yes, we heard. Joe has an idea where you are. We'll be there soon."

"Nate is Richard Bland," I said softly.

"We know. We heard. Where is he now? Are you all right?"

I stood on tiptoes and tried peeking over the rim of the floor. "I can't see him. I fell in a hole." I lowered my voice. "He's crazy. Absolutely bonkers."

"Cooperate with him. Whatever it takes. Understand?"

"Yes, but—"

"Give me the phone, Summer." I looked up. Richard was pointing a gun at my head. "Now."

What could I do? I handed it to him. "Now take my hand and let me pull you up."

"Okay." I dropped the blanket into the now ankle-deep water and grasped his hand.

Richard held the phone to his ear. "Banning, if you don't want anything to happen to your pretty little girlfriend, you'd better stay clear. Got it?" He closed the phone and turned to me. "You look like a drowned rat. Don't know what I ever saw in you."

"I don't care what you think of me, Richard. What am I now? Your hostage?"

He grasped my arm above the elbow. "Sounds good to me."

"Where are we going?"

"I haven't figured that part out yet." He yanked me through the door. "I'm in a bit of a predicament. I hadn't thought of taking a hostage. Puts me in really deep water."

And murder didn't? I was dealing with a child. We stepped off the porch, and I shrieked as lightning shot across the sky.

"Stop being a baby. I'm standing here with a gun. You're the hostage of a desperate man, and you're screaming about lightning?"

Good point. I straightened and allowed him to drag me to the car. A big, navy blue—something. I'd really have to study my car models. If I did manage to get free, Joe would ask me what kind of car Richard drove, guaranteed.

Richard opened the passenger door with the finesse of a football player and shoved me inside. My already aching head bounced off the seat. "Ow!"

"Sorry." He waved the ever-present gun in my face. "Stay put. You're useful as a hostage, but only if you behave."

"Yes, sir." I folded my arms across my chest and slouched in the seat. Having no idea where we were, it wouldn't do much good for me to run. My chance would come.

My captor slid behind the wheel and slung mud as we fishtailed away from the shack. We were still on the mountain, heading down. If Ethan and Joe didn't find me soon, we'd be near impossible to locate. My phone chirped, pulling me from my thoughts.

Richard pressed the speaker button with the tip of the gun. Always the careful driver, he kept one hand on the wheel. "Hello, Banning."

"Hodge, let Summer go. This is kidnapping."

"Oh, so it isn't Banning. Howdy, Officer Joe."

"Stop the car and let her go."

"It isn't kidnapping if you're taking a drive with your girl." Richard turned to me. "Aren't you my girl, Summer?"

I leaned closer to the phone. "We're heading down a mountain, Joe. I don't know which—" The back of Richard's hand connected with my mouth.

"Sorry, Joe. I've got to teach the lady some manners. We'll talk later." And the call ended.

Despair washed over me, landing on my shoulders like a black blanket. Heavy and suffocating. *Lord, what should I do? I can't overpower him. I don't know where we are. I need You to intervene. In a big way.*

Then peace washed over me with the force of a tsunami. Tears flowed, dripping off my chin and landing on my damp blouse.

My strength is sufficient. Wait, My child. Rescue will come.

"Are you crying? Stop it!" Richard pounded the steering wheel. Then he looked again. "Or are you smiling?"

I must have looked like a lunatic with a grin plastered across my face while the tears streamed. For the first time since I started on this crazy quest, I wasn't afraid. I'd sit back and take my opportunity when it presented itself.

"Sorry if my tears bother you, Richard. They're tears of joy. Of happiness. Full of God's love."

"Don't spout that nonsense at me." He turned the car right, heading west. The sun rose behind us, making this direction west, right? I never was any good at directions. Guess I'd have to take a class in navigation. Did anyone offer such a thing? I eyed the phone lying in the car's console.

"Don't even think about it. I'll shoot you in the hand."

"You're insane."

Wrong thing to say. Richard's eyes narrowed, and his face turned red. The words he spoke were as cold as ice. "Don't say that! All my life people have told me I was crazy. They sent me to that hospital. Doped me up." As he spoke, the volume of his words increased, and spittle flew from his chiseled lips as he shouted at me, "Mom wanted me committed. Did you know that?"

Go figure. "No, I didn't. I'm sorry." I scooted as far away from him as the door would allow. My gaze caught a sign. We were on Highway 40 headed west. Away from Arkansas and toward Oklahoma. I eyed the phone again.

Richard slowed to take the access road. In a fluid motion, I snatched the phone and flung open the door. Richard swerved the car, dumping me hard to the concrete. I rolled into a ditch, groaning from the pain of a bashed knee. I leaped to my feet and dashed into the trees.

22

Where to go? Where to go? My hair whipped around my face as I spun in a circle. *The phone.* I punched Ethan's number.

"Ethan! I'm free." I shoved aside some low-hanging branches as I pushed farther from the interstate. "I'm west on Interstate 40, mile marker 109. Hurry. He's coming after me."

Richard screamed my name. Twigs snapped behind me, propelling me forward.

"Can you find a place to hide?" Ethan's voice trembled.

"I'm trying. All I see are woods."

"We're coming, Summer. About twenty minutes."

A bullet ricocheted off a tree trunk. "You'd better hurry, Ethan. Otherwise, I'm a dead man, uh, woman." I screamed as another shot kicked up leaves at my feet.

"Step on it, Joe! He's shooting at her."

Come on, Summer. Look. There has to be a place to hide. I dropped the cell phone into my apron and sprinted to the right. My apron caught on a briar bush, slowing me before the fabric gave way and ripped. If I'd been able to escape on the mountain, I could've found a cave or overhang. Here in the flatland, I had limited choices.

Anything, God. A hollowed tree, a fallen stump. I'm not picky.

"Summer? Come out, come out, wherever you are." Richard's singsong voice carried to me through the trees and sent a shiver up my spine.

I stopped, panting, and listened. Not being the athletic type, this dash through the trees had winded me. I lifted a hand to my head and grimaced. A golf ball–sized goose egg took center stage on my forehead. Blood dried on my lip where Richard had slapped me, and my legs hurt. What else could possibly go wrong?

"I see you."

I whirled, brushing my flinging hair from my eyes. Where was he? If I couldn't see him, he couldn't see me, right? I snorted at reverting to the mentality of a three-year-old and darted to the left, slipping and sliding down a shallow hill.

At the bottom, a brook babbled. *Praise God!* I splashed in, the cool water soothing on my sore feet, and headed away from where Richard's call had cut through the trees. Had it been twenty minutes?

I reached for the cell phone in my apron pocket. It wasn't there. I must have dropped it when I slid down the hill. Guess that answered my question about what else could go wrong. I veered toward the interstate.

"Summer! Where are you?"

That wasn't Richard's voice. It was Ethan's. *Where*— I realized I held the phone in my left hand. I turned toward his voice and ran. "I'm here. Ethan, I'm here."

After a few yards, I burst through the bushes and onto the highway, yelping as I jumped back to avoid being hit by a speeding vehicle. My gaze searched in both directions. My heart leaped as I spotted the flashing lights of Joe's squad car. Ethan dashed off the road and headed toward the trees.

"Ethan! Joe!" My love turned to me. His eyes widened.

"Summer, drop!"

"What?" For once in my life, I obeyed. Officer Wayne emerged from the car, his weapon held at the ready. I fell to my knees as Joe raised his gun. Lying flat, I covered my head as they let loose a volley of shots.

Ethan ran to me and pulled me to my feet. "I thought I'd lost you."

I buried my face in his chest. "Never, Ethan. Never." I peeked beneath his arm to where Richard lay facedown on the asphalt. "He's crazy, you know."

"I know, sweetheart." Ethan raised my face and covered it with kisses. My insides warmed and flowed. His kisses were as sweet as the chocolate I loved to plunge my hands into. "Did you mean it? When you told Richard I was the only man for you?"

I could drown in his cobalt eyes. Tears escaped, running down the face I loved. "With all my heart."

Joe yanked me from Ethan's arms, engulfing me in a smothering hug. "Thought you were a goner for sure, little cuz."

With muffled words, I said, "I would've been, if not for your fine shooting, Joe. I owe you my life." I pulled back. "Thank you."

"Don't thank me. Thank that crazy man of yours. He wouldn't give up. Roused the whole town. When Aunt Eunice called and said you weren't where you were supposed to be—"

Man of mine. That sounded wonderful. The adrenaline must have worn off, because my legs refused to hold me any longer. Ethan looked at my face, hefted me in his arms, and marched to deposit me in the backseat of Joe's car.

"Call an ambulance, Joe."

"Already one on the way."

"I'm fine, Ethan." I tried brushing away his busy hands. Worried or not, I didn't know how long I could take his hands running over my body before I made a total fool of myself. "It's only a bump on the back of my head, another on my forehead, a split lip, and some bruises. Nothing that won't heal."

"Let me take care of you." He clasped my face in his hands. "I want to. Today, tomorrow, forever. As nuts as you make me, I want to spend the rest of my life with you."

I wasn't sure loving Ethan was what Aunt Eunice had been talking about, but I prayed that God's plan for my life included this man. I needed to be in his arms, and nowhere else. "Know what I want, Ethan?"

"Anything."

"Another of those lip-bruising kisses of yours." I smiled at him. "It was all I could think about when Nate pointed that gun at me. How I would miss receiving another one."

He lowered his head. I didn't get a lip-crushing kiss, but the tender one he planted on me would have melted the sun.

Cynthia is the mother of seven—three stepchildren, one birth child, and three adopted children. She has five grandchildren. She grew up as an army "brat," living in California, Oklahoma, and Germany, with most of her childhood spent in the small town of Atkins, Arkansas, in the foothills of the Ozark Mountains.

Cynthia grew up in a family of storytellers. For years she sat around and listened while her grandmother or an aunt or uncle told her stories of their family's history. As she grew, she learned some of the stories were true, while others were just that—stories. Storytelling is in her blood, and she can't imagine doing anything else.

You may correspond with this author by writing:
Cynthia Hickey
Author Relations
PO Box 721
Uhrichsville, OH 44683

A Letter to Our Readers

Dear Reader:
In order to help us satisfy your quest for more great mystery stories, we would appreciate it if you would take a few minutes to respond to the following questions. We welcome your comments and read each form and letter we receive. When completed, please return to:

Fiction Editor
Heartsong Presents—MYSTERIES!
PO Box 721
Uhrichsville, Ohio 44683

Did you enjoy reading *Fudge-Laced Felonies* by Cynthia Hickey?

Very much! I would like to see more books like this! The one thing I particularly enjoyed about this story was:

_____

_____

_____

Moderately. I would have enjoyed it more if:

_____

_____

_____

Are you a member of the HP—MYSTERIES! Book Club?
Yes No

If no, where did you purchase this book?

_____

Please rate the following elements using a scale of 1 (poor) to 10 (superior):

___ Main character/sleuth   ___ Romance elements

___ Inspirational theme   ___ Secondary characters

___ Setting   ___ Mystery plot

How would you rate the cover design on a scale of 1 (poor) to 5 (superior)? _____

What themes/settings would you like to see in future **Heartsong Presents—MYSTERIES!** selections? _____

_____

_____

_____

Please check your age range:
      Q Under 18   Q 18–24
      Q 25–34   Q 35–45
      Q 46–55   Q Over 55

Name: _____

Occupation: _____

Address: _____

E-mail address: _____

Heartsong Presents

Any 8 Titles for $32! A 20% Savings!

Great Mysteries at a Great Price! Purchase Any Title for Only $4.97 Each!

HEARTSONG PRESENTS—MYSTERIES!
TITLES AVAILABLE NOW:

— MYSTERIES! —

Heartsong Presents—MYSTERIES! provide romance and faith interwoven among the pages of these fun whodunits. Written by the talented and brightest authors in this genre, such as Christine Lynxwiler, Cecil Murphey, Nancy Mehl, Dana Mentink, Candice Speare, and many others, these cozy tales are sure to challenge your mind, warm your heart, touch your spirit—and put your sleuthing skills to the test.

Not all titles may be available at time of order.
If outside the U.S., please call
740-922-7280 for shipping charges.

OHIO
Weddings

3 stories in 1

Secrets, love, and danger are afoot when three remarkable women reexamine their lives on Bay Island. Lauren Wright returns to straighten out her past only to disrupt her future. Becky Merrill steps onto the shore and into sabotage. Judi Rydell can't outrun her former life. Who will rescue their hearts?

ISBN 978-1-59789-987-1
Contemporary, paperback, 352 pages 5³⁄₁₆" x 8"

A BRIDE SO FAIR

Emily Ralston is delighted when she lands a job at the Children's Building at the World's Fair. When a lost boy is found by a handsome guard and soon after a dead body turns up, the mystery begins to unfold. Can Emily deliver little Adam to safety before time runs out?

ISBN 978-1-59789-492-0
288 pages, $10.97

Mississippi
WEDDINGS

3 stories in 1

Romance rocks the lives of three women in Magnolia Bay. Meagan Evans's heart is torn between two men. Ronni Melrose meets a man determined to break down her defenses. Dani Phillips is caught in a raging storm—within and without. Can these three women ride out the wave of love?

Contemporary, paperback, 352 pages, 5³/₁₆" x 8"

Florida WEDDINGS

3 stories in 1

The past casts a shadow upon the lives of three women. When Renee Austin's firm is ransacked, she's deemed the culprit. Jeris Waldron is still reeling from an abusive relationship. Bethany Hamilton feels safe in Florida—until she comes face-to-face with the man who once abandoned her. Can these women find the strength and faith to embrace the future?

Contemporary, paperback, 352 pages, 5³/₁₆" x 8"
